THE WORLD OF AVIS BLACKTHORN

The illustrated guide of books 1, 2, 3 & prequel

JACK SIMMONDS

INTRODUCTION

I started writing Avis Blackthorn in October 2014. I had just received my fortieth rejection letter from another large London based publishing house for a book I had taken a few years to write. This wasn't working. If I wanted to be a writer full time then I had to change my methods and embrace the new ways of doing things — self-publishing.

So I decided to write a new book and gave myself six months to write it (not two years). I had an idea written in my notebook about a wizard who lived with an evil family. It made me laugh, so I thought that was a good place to start. Originally, while working on it, it was titled: "The Diary of a Cr*p Wizard". That name wasn't going to work. So I thought about names for the main character.

I had this albino budgie at home called Avis. He was a funny bird who would always come and sit on your finger when you clicked and he would hang upside down from the light fitting and chew the picture frames. He was a nutter. My sister also told me that Avis meant magic in latin, or something. So I settled on that.

For the surname, I wanted something that summarised the characters — they are evil and they are quite prickly in their personalities, so *black* and *thorns* went together well. Blackthorn.

I also didn't want them to just be plain evil, there has to be a reasons and a motive for choosing to be evil — perhaps they didn't choose for example (shh, mustn't give anything else away).

Then, the idea of the magic school came to me. I thought *if I could re-write Harry Potter, how would I have done it?* I didn't want it to be a copy or a fan-fiction of Harry Potter, not at all. So I had to make wholesale changes to the way things worked at Hailing Hall. But I do draw comparison between the relationship of Harry and Malfoy — Avis would be Malfoy: part of an evil family with certain things expected from him and Jasper would be Harry Potter, the respected but flawed *saviour*.

The first book was more of a success that I thought it would be and is even on sale at Wallmart in America. As a Brit, that's pretty cool. My plan is to write a 8 books in the series, but that depends on what will happen after Avis, Robin and Tina finish school and how the story is to unfold. I already know the ending, *muhahaha*. And no, I won't tell you.

ABOUT ME

I was born in a place called Enfield in the north of London, UK. When I was ten my parents and I moved to the darkest depths of the countryside to a place by the sea-side. It was a great place to grow up, to go out on bicycles all day, knock for friends and have a merry old time. At school I was naughty and cheeky. I got sent out of lessons a lot, but I was never suspended or anything like that, I just prized being funny above learning French.

I went to Bath Spa University and studied Acting — yes, I

originally wanted to be an actor in films and even moved back to London for a while to try and break into that industry, all the while I was writing my books.

ABOUT THIS BOOK

This has taken a long time to write, illustrate and put together. It takes a long time to invent a new world and even longer to draw it. From the characters, to the kingdoms, the flying carriages, the food, the ghosts, the magic, the rules, the mysteries and history, the creatures, the magical animals and everything else in between that makes a world the rich tapestry that it is takes a long and painstaking time. So I hope you enjoy this book.

The illustrations and annotations are from books 1, 2 and some from the Prequel.

ABOUT MAGDA

I'm from Poland. I finished Cultural Studies in specialising in visual communication and graphic design.

I am very interested in illustrations, storyboarding and animation, which I practise in my free time.

I am the author of the ongoing webcomic Timeriders (http://timeriderscomic.blogspot.com/)

ABOUT MAGDA AND I

Magda and I started working together a few months after the first Avis Blackthorn was released. I got someone online to do me a cover, and it did the job for a while, but I wanted something that would stand out more. I scoured art and illustration sites online to find a talented illustrator, that's when I stumbled across Magda's work. I messaged her and we started working together right away. What impressed me was how passionate Magda is about her work. She, like me, prizes and enjoys her craft.

I just hope she sticks around until I publish the last book!

I

THE BLACKTHORNS

AVIS BLACKTHORN

"From the outside you would think my family exceptionally strange. They pride themselves on being the most evil family in all of the Seven Magical Kingdoms, a title which no one is due to question. We, the Blackthorns, are pretty notorious."

BIRTHDAY: 14th April.

  Favourite food: Trifle (or apricot croissants)

  Height: 5"1

He is small for his age, by his own admission and has, according his mother a "sloped, unsymmetrical face" — but perhaps she was just being cruel for the sake of it. When Avis looks in the mirror, he doesn't think he looks that bad. Sometimes he wishes he had some cool, stand out feature like a two different coloured eyes, or a streak of white through his hair, but instead he looks like most other teenagers. Except for the rather embarrassing fact that he has... in a place you wouldn't expect either... on his bottom is... a birthmark of the number 7.

Strange huh?

HIS BIRTHDAY IS in mid April, although he often forgets, due to the fact that all through his upbringing everyone purposefully forgot. Or would at least tease or give him a booby trapped present.

There was a time when Avis opened a present, with his whole family watching on. He was very apprehensive as he half-expected something to explode and take his head off. But instead, it was a small puppy dog. It yapped and licked his face. Avis was most confused, he had always wanted a puppy, a best friend, but he never thought his parents would allow it. They all grinned as Avis thanked them profusely and ran around the castle with it, while his parents gave evil looks to whoever had bought him it.

It was at the end of an exhausting day playing with the puppy, when Avis was laying in bed with it curled up on his lap, when the clock struck midnight when the little puppy started to morph and change, growing fast. Avis opened his eyes, and blinked unbelieving, as the puppy was now as tall as the ceiling — and it was not a puppy anymore, it was a murderous looking wolf with razor sharp teeth with slime dripping out of it's mouth.

"RWOOOF!" It went, teeth bared and ready to attack. Avis

slid off his bed and slid underneath as fast as he could as the giant wolf snapped at him. Avis lay crying under the bed, one for the loss of his lovely puppy and the other because he didn't want to die.

There was a chorus of laughter from downstairs that Avis could hear. They knew. They were watching in their Crystal Balls.

"It's a ware-puppy! I stole it from it's mother in the haunted forest!" Rory cried his voice magically flooding into the room, as all Avis's siblings laughed along. "It will change back soon!"

"WHEN?!" Avis cried.

"Next full moon..."

"Next full moon?!" Avis screeched. "I can't stay under here til next full moon!"

Before Avis went to Hailing Hall School for Wizards, he attended *Foogle Furgo's Magial Therory School*, just up the road from Darkampton. He didn't like it there at all — he was always very lonely. Because he was a Blackthorn, no one wanted to be his friend. They were all terrified of him. But this also meant that no one bullied him either, so he was always left completely on his own. Avis struggled through these years, sometimes he made a friend or two, usually new people to the school and they would soon twig that they should not hang around him. Avis held onto the fact that very soon he would be starting at Hailing Hall, a boarding school for other young wizards. For ages and ages he would fantasise about being someone completely different and made up new names for himself, so no one could hate him for being a Blackthorn.

Henry Hawkins.
William Grewball.

Or perhaps something really normal sounding, like Charlie Smith?

But he had a problem — his brother Ross would be in his last year at Hailing Hall when Avis would start his first year. And Ross would make extra sure they everyone knew Avis was a Blackthorn.

Bummer.

AVIS'S LIFE GROWING UP

This is the problem: the Blackthorns are quite possibly, the most evil family in all of the Seven Magical Kingdoms. But Avis is not evil at all, he couldn't, and wouldn't hurt a fly. He is the black sheep in the Blackthorn family, shunned to the side while the evil people got on with their evil tasks.

Avis knows full well that he is a big disappointment to his parents so he tries to keep out of their way. Otherwise they may get ideas about *making him evil*. Something Avis has experienced many times, his parents lofty ideas and schemes to force the evil in him out. But always to no avail.

Avis lives with his parents in their castle Darkhampton, which is dark, draughty and smells. The castle is in the grounds of Happendance, which one of the sunniest, prettiest kingdoms — but Avis doesn't like it much. He describes it as *"the second worst, after Farkingham, which is just a black dustbowl..."*

One plus, is that Darkhampton is so large that Avis could sleep in a different bedroom every night for a year if he so pleased. Obviously he wouldn't do that, because there could be anything lurking in some of those rooms. He had almost been eaten alive by a very hungry Mardilo once, when he got lost on the way to the toilet. A Mardilo is a tall bear like creature around eight feet tall with razor sharp teeth. He only just managed to survive by summoning his wardrobe, which landed on top of the Mardilo with a splat!

SEDRICK

Avis's best friend growing up was his fluffy rabbit Sedrick which went everywhere with him — except when his siblings were in the castle, as they may try and rip his head off or something.

There was a funny old time in the summer holidays a few weeks before he started at Hailing Hall, when he accidentally brought Sedrick to life! His parents left a very valuable magical item on the table: the Ring of Enchantment. Avis, thinking *what harm could it do?* used it. Sedrick came alive and started walking and talking... Avis's dream come true! But then, the worst thing happened... Sedrick ran away!

From *Avis Blackthorn and the Ring of Enchantment*

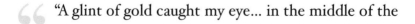 "A glint of gold caught my eye... in the middle of the

table, in a small, black box, was a small golden ring. But not just any ring, I knew what this was... it was the Ring of Enchantment!

This was one of the most prized possessions in the magical world. My parents had gone to extraordinary measures to get it — heaven forbid whoever got in their way. I remember peering through the bannisters one night when my parents returned. They couldn't see me, I was hidden behind a statue, but anyway, they were talking about it and I saw them wave it around — they said it enchanted things to come alive! Which, they thought would be very useful — if they needed information about where someone may have gone, they can enchant a stone to come alive and ask it where so and so went. Or, so they reckoned anyway.

I lent forwards and plucked it out of the box, twirling it round in my hand I saw on the inside of the ring it read: *Ring of Enchantment. Use Wisely.*"

"I shut the door of my room and locked it. Stupid Kilkenny. I went and sat on my bed and pulled out the ring, laying back and twirling it round in my hand. I was holding The Ring of Enchantment.

Sedrick, my fluffy rabbit teddy, lay to my left. Suddenly, something brilliant crept across my mind...

I was always complaining about not having any friends. Sedrick was my only friend, but he was just a small bag of cotton and fluff, he wasn't alive. But he could be...

They wouldn't notice would they? I'd just make him come alive, then tell him to pretend to not be enchanted when anyone was around. It was the perfect plan! Finally, I would bring my best friend to life!

But how did I do it? I had no idea. I lay Sedrick in the middle of the stone floor and stood over him.

I put the ring on, it fitted my middle finger perfectly. Which was strange. But, I had no idea what to do... hec, what was I thinking? This wasn't going to work. I was twelve years old and knew hardly any magic and this was one of the most powerful magical objects ever made. This was the ring that was infamous in Wizarding folk-lore for belonging to Wizard Hermanus and his apprentice Jermain who stole it and caused a catastrophe with hundreds of broomsticks turning murderous.

"Huh," I sighed glumly going to twist the ring off. "I just wish you'd come alive..." before I could twist it all the way off, something happened. There was a spark of golden light that licked the air like a matchstick spark. Then, all of a sudden, blinding white light nearly threatened to blast me off my feet! It erupted throughout the room like a bomb — then, silence.

When the light faded, I looked down. Sedrick stood blinking. He was alive!

"Sedrick?" I said as torrents of amazement flooded through me. I couldn't believe it, he was actually alive! Sedrick blinked again and looked around his fluffy body, then looked up at me.

"Hello Avis..." he had a soft voice, just how I'd imagined..."

AVIS HAD to go to extraordinary measures to get the ring back, which you can read about in the book. But needless to say it was an epic adventure to find and rescue his best friend — Sedrick. When Avis goes off to school in his first year, he makes sure to hide Sedrick in a crack in the floor so no one can find him and do something horrible to him. In the second year Avis uses magic to hide Sedrick in an alcove, covering it with shadow.

2

THE BLACKTHORN FAMILY

This is Wendice and Rory Blackthorn.

"[They are] ashamed of me because I am not inherently *evil* like they are. My Mum is a hard woman, not one to cross. She's a terribly fierce witch who works constantly. I have three older sisters, almost identical to her in looks and personality. Then there's my six older brothers, all terribly handsome, fiercely competitive and unashamedly evil."

NIGEL AND GWENDOLINE BLACKTHORN

Nigel and Gwendoline Blackthorn are Avis's parents. They are both very tall, upright and powerful people. They work directly for Malakai, doing his bidding and run what's called The Organisation — they hold meetings, organise raids and further what they call '*the cause*.'

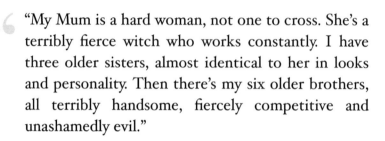

"My Mum is a hard woman, not one to cross. She's a terribly fierce witch who works constantly. I have three older sisters, almost identical to her in looks and personality. Then there's my six older brothers, all terribly handsome, fiercely competitive and unashamedly evil."

"My brothers were all in a corner doing mini-duels until Dad came over, his presence enough to make them scatter. Dad is a cool guy, and an impressive figure. Standing over six feet tall, with a stare that could topple a giant elephant, he always dresses smartly, and has recently grown a beard which suits him. I like my Dad — I just wish he liked me. People in the party treat him with reverence, while others are jealous of the trust that Malakai has in him, I just know it."

HIS SIBLINGS

The siblings have spread themselves across the Seven Magical Kingdoms — this is intentional, so they can keep their ears to the ground and report back to their parents any findings.

> "Our family is strange you see, their evilness has led to several strange traits: Marianne lives in the sunniest part of the Seven Kingdoms and has a palace with a glass roof that she calls Crystal Palace. It gets near twenty hours a day sunlight — she loves it. My parents however, love darkness. My brother's Wilson and Simon love the cold, and live in a big ice castle in Slackerdown. Wendice loves silence and

darkness, and lives in a sound proofed palace in Farkingham. Whereas Gertrude loves noise, shouting, parties and dances and her palace in Golandria, has a permanent dancing troupe, band and party guests. It's a flipping strange family, this one."

MARIANNE

Marianne is the most flamboyant out of all Avis's sisters and the loudest. She is also the most driven to succeed with her evilness. She even goes so far as to use quite the arsenal of love spells to trick and marry Edward Burrows, son of the Djinn who Avis releases in his second year at Hailing Hall, so that they can tie the Blackthorns and the Burrows (a wealthy and important magical family) together.

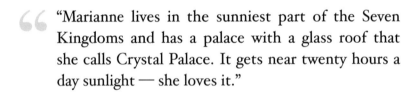

"Marianne lives in the sunniest part of the Seven Kingdoms and has a palace with a glass roof that she calls Crystal Palace. It gets near twenty hours a day sunlight — she loves it."

WENDICE

Wendice (*pic. above*) is a dark haired witch with looks very much like her mothers. But she is quite reserved and cunning, this is proven when she fights with Gertrude over a blue dress before setting it alight causing Gertrude to run away crying.

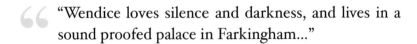

"Wendice loves silence and darkness, and lives in a sound proofed palace in Farkingham..."

"Wendice stood about smugly, waving her dress,

before announcing: "You know actually I think she was right, I don't think I like it," with a click of her fingers, the blue dress caught fire and she dropped it on the floor, where it burned to a blue dust. "I'm going to find something nicer for the wedding." She flounced off back the way she came smiling to herself. Wendice had changed — last year she was as fat as Gertrude, but now she was skinnier than me, with long hair and a golden complexion. It was quite a transformation. She was already saying she'd had twelve proposals for marriage."

GERTRUDE

Gertrude is the fattest of all three sisters who has not sorted herself out like the other two have. When they were all fat and ugly, they were nicknamed the *ugly sisters* — but when old enough, Marianne used magic to make herself as attractive as one could, losing weight and adopting a glamorous complexion. For some reason Gertrude hasn't got round to it yet.

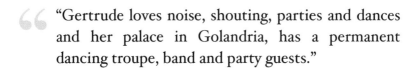

"Gertrude loves noise, shouting, parties and dances and her palace in Golandria, has a permanent dancing troupe, band and party guests."

"I follow fat Gertrude, her wobbly bottom barely fitting inside a huge blue dress. I thought about telling her that she needn't worry if she falls down the long stone spiral staircase, because she'll have an equivalent of about fifty cushions to soften the fall. I don't, just in case she sits on me and squashes me to death.

The party was just as I expected, lots of horrible

people I know I hate who all look at me and smile gleefully as Gertrude announces my arrival, while stuffing three eclairs in her big wobbly gob."

WILSON & SIMON

"Wilson looked like a dog with a smashed in face, due to a fight with a Wolfraptor. He wore blood red ceremonial gowns with gold trimmings... I rather thought he looked like a baboon in a cape. Simon was simple, very simple, when he looks at you there's clearly nothing much there. He's dead behind the eyes and brainless — slime always drips from the corner of his mouth and his choice of clothes is beyond strange. Today's selection is: chrome trousers with a neon yellow shirt and pastel green trimmings. All the brains went to Harold, he is exceptionally clever and cunning, I would never, ever decide on him as an enemy — he's the one sibling I am most scared of."

WILSON & Simon live together and are very similar. They are both dopy, dim and trusted very little by their family other than to fight. As Avis states, "all the brains went to Harold..."

"Wilson looked like a dog with a smashed in face, due to a fight with a Wolfraptor. He wore blood red ceremonial gowns with gold trimmings... I rather thought he looked like a baboon in a cape."

Wilson has a brash and unpredictable personality owing to the fact that he has always felt undervalued by the family — he would often find them having secret meetings without him. This annoyed him profusely, as he thought all his ideas were brilliant. Wilson and Simon live together as their parents do not trust Simon on his own, being a little bit dim as he is.

> "My brother's Wilson and Simon love the cold, and live in a big ice castle in Slackerdown."

Wilson and Simon regard living in the coldest Kingdom as a badge of honour — they insist it makes them tougher, and will not let the servants light fires in the castle, which means they are constantly going through staff.

> "Simon was simple, very simple, when he looks at you there's clearly nothing much there. He's dead behind the eyes and brainless — slime always drips from the corner of his mouth and his choice of clothes is beyond strange..."

HAROLD

Harold is the oldest and cleverest of all Avis's siblings. He brings a calmness, a charisma and a sense of purpose that make their parents glad that they will be leaving the family name up to him, the eldest and cleverest.

> "All the brains went to Harold, he is exceptionally clever and cunning, I would never, ever decide on him as an enemy — he's the one sibling I am most scared of."

Harold becomes a main player in Avis life in his second year at Hailing Hall. He takes the role of Infusions Magisteer at the school. Avis thinks that this is to keep an eye on him and to spy. Harold denies this, even though he would regard the post at Hailing Hall as a step down in terms of his professional career — he's capable of far greater.

RORY

Rory (*pic. above*) is not as clever as Harold, in his mid-twenties he is moderately successful, running his own evil shop on the outskirts of the shopping town Gnippoh's, selling cursed furniture, weapons and interesting things that only evil people would use.

He took over the running of the shop from Great Uncle Farrybold (more on him later) who left his shop to the family, but no one had the time to run it. So Rory took it over and changed it from a well respected antique furniture shop, to a place where only evil people would frequent.

GARY

Gary sometimes helps out Rory, but like Simon, he is not blessed in the brains department, but makes up for it with good looks and flits arounds between his brothers and sisters castles, never staying for longer than a few weeks before leaving. He loves parties and meeting new princesses. He falls in love very easily. He wants to own his own castle soon, but he cannot work out what he wants to do with his life. So settles for being a full time party-goer.

ROSS

> "Ross is closest to me in age, still lives at home with me and is the bane of my life."

Ross is closest to Avis is age, and has most of an effect on Avis in his first year at school. In the Chamber on the first day when Avis is trying to make a good impression and make friends, before he realises that Ross has done magic to make all Avis' most embarrassing moments flash up upon his robes — Avis runs out crying. But if he had not, then Avis would never have met Tina, so on balance, Avis would probably say it was for the best.

GREAT UNCLE FARRYBOLD

Great Uncle Farrybold was an eccentric man, who like Avis, was not particularly evil — which in an evil family like the Blackthorns is a bit of a problem. However, his sister, Gwendoline (Avis's Mother) looked after him. He lived in the castle with them until quite recently.

> "Partington taught us all about enchanted furniture, which I found fascinating. I contributed to the class in fact, because my Great Uncle Farrybold, who lived with us until a year ago when he passed over, was an eccentric antique dealer and was always bringing home huge bits of furniture, like sofa's that sprouted unlimited seats, wardrobes that chose your outfit for the day and even a hairbrush that grew back hair on bald men (it didn't work on him). He was killed by an antique billiards table in the end,

which collapsed on him when he said a trigger word. It was a shame, he was always nice to me, when he remembered who I was."

BUTLER KILKENNY

Butler Kilkenny is the family's resident Butler. He is very old and creaks around the castle at a very slow speed. They really should get rid of him and replace him with a newer model. Avis often wonders why they don't? And just get a nice Butler, but he heard his parents talking and saying it would be hard to find a Butler that would put up with the family. So they put a life extension charm on him without his knowledge.

He has been in the family since he was young and was their Grandparents servant, being in the family now for three generations.

Born in Cork, Ireland, he stumbled into the magical world by complete accident. He came over to England when he was 19 to start work in a country manor house... except he got lost, and traipsed across the countryside looking for it, before stumbling through a thick hedge row and finding himself in the grounds of Darkhampton. Happy to find what he assumed was the manor house at last, he rushed inside and soon discovered that it was not the one he meant to be working at. However, the Blackthorns were very accommodating and gave him a job immediately.

It was over the next few weeks that he discovered magic was real and that these people were Wizards. He tried to escape several times, but was always caught and brought back — they couldn't let him leave, he knew too much.

3

THE ENGAGEMENT PARTY

"I watched from my new hiding spot, just inside an alcove in the wall hidden by shadow, and observed these *evil* people, who, in some way or another were kind of ugly. I recognised quite a lot of faces from the Malakai meetings. There were Warlords and Warlocks, Pig-people, loads of Wicked Witches with their black cats and broomsticks, (yes, the stories are correct)."

As you can see from this image, just before the party starts — we have green drinks (rotten apple punch) and cake with blood icing with eyeballs on, goodness only knows where they got that from. The witch is enchanted and made out of ice — she dances in a slow rhythmic fashion, before people break bits off her and put them in their drinks.

This scene is before the party really starts, but it gives you an idea of the work that goes into such an event. The Blackthorns are well known through the Seven Magical Kingdoms and have guests that include Kings, Queens, Ministers and such like, so a good impression must be made on all.

"Then my brothers found me. Creeping up on me by disguising themselves as the wall, they think they are so clever with their Magic. I knew they were up to something as soon as I saw them, they had that evil glint in their eye - too much rotten apple punch for a start.

"What do you want?" I said.

"Oh Avis," said Rory, the oldest. "That's no way to talk to your beloved brothers."

"Yeah, we just want some fun," said Gary smiling malevolently, he was known for his evil smile.

Rory, Ross and Gary held my shoulder and stood me up while Larry and Stan chuckled behind.

Rory winked at me. "Were gonna make you evil Avis..."

I sighed, there was no use getting out of this. There were six of them who could all do Magic, against one of me, who couldn't.

They stood with me at the food table, Rory stayed close, whispering in my ear. "Right, grab that big bowl of trifle."

I did, too weary not to comply.

"And..." Rory chuckled then signalled to the others.

With a flick of their fingers, the bowl left my hands and flew into the air. It sailed right across the room to where Wendice stood. The trifle splattered all the way up her back as the crowd went stony silent. I turned, heart in my mouth, but my brothers had resumed to being a grey shade of wall. All eyes fell on me."

THIS IS PRETTY NORMAL — Avis just knew that something like that would happen. His brothers just love to play tricks on him. They have an advantage, they are brilliant at magic, while Avis can't use any yet. So they make a whole bowl of trifle sail across the room and fly up Marianne's back.

❧ 4 ❧

AVIS RETURNS HOME

When he returns from his first year at Hailing Hall, his parents make him clean the castle which Avis is obviously not happy about. The wedding of the year between Marianne and Edward Burrows is due to take place and the castle must be in ship-shape for all the guests that will arriving from all over the magical Kingdoms.

"Right now, I am scrubbing the floor high up in one of the twelve turrets. It's absolutely filthy! I mean black with dirt. I doubt it's ever been cleaned. This is not a voluntary decision either, I am being held at spell-point, practically, by my parents who need the castle to be in ship shape ready for a thousand or so guests to turn up for the wedding of the bloody year. My sister Marianne and her poor deluded Prince finance are getting married in the grounds of our castle *Darkhampton*. She has him under a love spell I just know it. My parents encourage them who to marry — usually rich and influential families to increase their own reach and power."

It's not uncommon to be treated like a slave by his own family — this has connotations to Cinderella, who was treated like a slave by her family...

> "I felt like Cinderella, being treated like a slave! Mind you, I could do what she did... sue her family and live in comfort for the rest of her life on the settlement. Apparently it bankrupted that family and they all had to move into a council flat with relatives on the *Outside*. I imagined my parents all living in a tiny flat after I sued them for mistreatment. I held onto this fuzzy dream as I scrubbed and scrubbed."

But it's during this time that something strange happens. Avis finds Ross cleaning up high in the castle too — this puzzles Avis because Ross was one of his parents favourites, what had he done to make them ask him to clean too? When Avis spots him Ross goes mad at Avis saying that it was all his fault! Just in the nick of time, the Seven League Shoes kick in and Avis shoots away on a bed of golden light... straight into... a strange and dark turret he'd never seen or been to before...

"My Granddad sat as still as a rusty nail, and looked as gnarled and grizzled as one. His face scarred and lined, due to all the fights he'd had. But all in all, for a dead person he looked pretty good — dressed in long black day clothes and a navy blue cape. His magical cane stood next to his chair, small colourful lights fizzing just under the surface. I was always fascinated by it as a kid and could watch for hours. We sat in silence for a long time, my mouth open, just staring at him."

His Granddad proceeds to gift Avis a very special, golden

pendant channeller with a strange mark on it. As we have come to know, this mark is known as the 'Mark of the Seventh Son' — Malakai draws it on the wall in his room up high in Hailing Hall, Jasper has the same mark on his pendant channeller and it's also on the incense holder that contained the Djinn, Burrows, who is also a seventh son.

The strangest thing about the whole encounter was that his Granddad was supposed to be dead.

A DARING ESCAPE

AVIS IS MADE to be a waiter at the wedding and gets to watch on as it takes place. Unbeknownst to him, and everyone else there, people are sitting in wait to disrupt the wedding. People dressed all in white, one of whom tries to chase after Avis who manages to escape by running through the castle. This man turns out to be Burrows assistant Chambers — the man Marianne is marrying is Edward Burrows, his son.

So Avis manages to pack some things while the fight escalated outside and runs through the kitchens to the courtyard at the back of the castle and into a carriage — his brothers try and shoot the carriage down with him inside it! But he manages to evade them...

> "The carriage sailed into the white dot. I shielded my eyes before seeing green grass and brown earth, before falling, faster and faster. I clung on for dear life as the carriage seemed to lose all power and careered for the ground.
>
> "*AHHHH!*" I cried in vain as I braced myself for the inevitable.
>
> *CRAAAAASSSSHHHHH!* We smashed into ground, casting mud and earth into the air from all around as a sickening *eeeeeekkkkkkkk* sound erupted from all around. I flew to the front and face planted the glass. I heard a sickening crunching noise, then pain, glorious, horrible, stinging pain! The carriage skidded through earth, before flipping over and over and over... me and my bag turning summersaults as it repeatedly smacked into my already sore face. I grabbed it as we span, round and round like some tortuous fairground ride. I preyed for it to be over already. Then, the carriage turned upside down, my body rose into the middle of the

carriage in one glorious floating moment... before the leather seat, all at once, came crashing into my midriff, winding me completely — and then all was still, as darkness set in. I couldn't help close my eyes, and let my aching body rest.

The pain echoed through my body even in sleep. When my eyes finally opened, all I could see was a pounding white light in front of my eyes where my nose throbbed. All down the front of my jacket was blood. All over the carriage roof, or floor, was blood. I blinked and sat up. The carriage was upside down in, from what I could make out from the gap in the window that wasn't buried in mud, the middle of a field. My stomach groaned as I sat forwards, the winding I received coming back in painful spurts like invisible stabbing needles. The carriage was making a weird whizzing sound and emitting a large amount of purple smoke, I had to get out of here quickly. With my head throbbing, and nose crying, I lent round and kicked the carriage door. Every pore of my body begged me to stop, as the pain rippled around me. *Stop being such a wuss,* I said to myself, hoping that it could make the pains just sod off. I gave another kick and caught the window which smashed. Purple smoke began billowing out of the carriage as if it was a race. Kicking the glass out of the panel I crawled out through the small gap, catching my robes on the shards and hearing small tearing sounds. But I didn't care, I was out of the carriage at last and... in the middle of a big field."

5

FRIENDS

ROBIN WILSON

Birthday: 24th July
    Favourite food: Sausages and mash
    Height: 5"9

As well as being very tall for his age, and *lanky* (like a lamp-post, as Avis puts it) Robin is also a very good and loyal friend. Many people would have given up with Avis if put through the same amount of stress — and the reputation Avis comes with, being a Blackthorn, is enough to put anyone off.

Seeing Avis allegedly call a demon upon Hunter, in their first year at Hailing Hall, was the first time Avis and Robin came to blows and Robin denounced Avis as a friend, but later he soon comes to realise that it couldn't have been Avis, and sets out to help him in his battle against Malakai.

In their second year, he argues with Avis about him not making a wish with the Djinn in the incense holder, but Avis ignores his advice. But when the bite in the tail of the wish takes hold, he helps Avis instead of telling him *I told you so,* saving his life yet again.

Robin assumed, at the end of his last term at his old school that he would go to the nearest school 'Gravels Comprehensive' just up the road from his parents house, in Yorkshire with his best friend Geoff. But over the summer holidays many strange occurrences gave Robin the impression that something was trying to get his attention. Whether it be the strange man that turned up to his door, asked specifically for Robin and tried to sell him some strange jewellery. Or the strange multicoloured insect that flew through his open window and into his bedroom — the likes of which he had never seen before in his life. Or the TV crackling one night and interrupting his favourite programme with some strange news programme, presented by people in triangular hats talking about magic. Or, while out shopping for new school clothes with his parents; seeing three teenagers watching him from afar, dressed strangely in cloaks and muttering amongst each other. Then, after walking away to find his parents, there was an ungodly sound as a brand new shop popped into existence in-between the two that were already there — and no one even noticed! In a flash, the man who owned this shop that just appeared out of nowhere tried to hustle Robin into the shop and tried to sell him some strange coloured robes. Robin pushed him away and ran out the shop after his parents.

Robin would have thought that he was going mad, if it were not all explained to him by two people who came striding through his garden the next day and proceeded to tell him all about magic, Hailing Hall and the fact that he was a Wizard. These two people told his parents that Robin had been chosen to go to an exceptionally special *spy school* on behalf on the British Government. They seemed appeased and allowed him to go.

You could mistake Robin for being a bit of a geek, who loves to read and do his homework. He was the spelling champion of his previous school before he went to Hailing Hall. But he has a mischievous and ambitious side to him — he, as well as his other Condor form mates were unhappy about losing their first ever game of Riptide, but unlike the others, he wanted to do something about it and stop the teasing. So he, Hunter and Avis dress up as Malakai to scare the living daylights out of the Eagles form — to teach them a lesson! Needless to say, it all goes pear-shaped (*see comment above about the demon*).

OR IN SECOND YEAR, when Avis convinced him to wear his special spectacles to play Riptide — this would allow him to be able to see the special Ornaments that allowed one to gain power-ups through the match.

Or the countless times they evade the school rules and break into the library late at night to do some studying... first and second years are only permitted to look at a few books, the rest are barred (for their own safety) so the only time they would be able to see those books is when the library is empty at night.

ROBIN BECOMES EXASPERATED with Avis throughout their first years at Hailing Hall. Avis desperately wants to prove himself as a good wizard, that he is not evil like his family. Fortunately, he has a friend in Robin that understands and is empathetic to Avis's cause. Through the first year they get along fairly well, until the incident with Hunter and Malakai. But then Robin saves Avis's life by bringing him back to life using the Book of Names. Everyone involved, including Tina, Ernie, Magisteer Partington, Robin and Avis made a pact not to reveal the truth. This magical pact will do bad things if broken.

Robin originally attached himself to Avis in a bid find out more about the magical world, finding it fascinating, being an Outsider. But over time they become inseparable.

He also maintained friends with Graham, the Scottish boy in his form who was also from the Outside and together had many discussions about how strange it was that they should find themselves in the magical lands — but being young, they were adaptable. Robin spent a lot of his time with Graham and Simon during the period that Avis is ostracised.

THE FIRST TIME AVIS MEETS ROBIN

"My eyes opened. I was on the train. It was just a dream! Thank goodness for that, I hated snakes. But there was someone standing over me and prodding my arm.

"Hello?" he said again.

I rubbed my eyes and looked around. The boy was tall, wire thin and spoke with this funny accent from your world - the north of England somewhere, I saw a programme about it.

"Erm, hi?" I said, noticing I was still on the train

and it was nearly dark! "Oh no! I haven't missed Hailing Station have I?"

"What? Naa, that's why I was waking ya..." he said, his little beady eyes blinking nervously behind thick glass frames. "To ask if you were going to Hailing Hall school too?"

"What?" I was genuinely surprised, somehow I didn't expect to see anyone else going to Hailing Hall on the train. His beady little eyes looked down at me through the comical little circular spectacles. "Yeah I am, are you?"

"Yeah, the stop's soon, thought I'd let ya know. Don't wanna sleep through and miss ya' first day o' school."

"No exactly."

I stood and stretched, the carriage now empty. My pockets felt oddly empty too. With a sinking feeling, I put my hands in them to check, all my gold pieces had gone! I would have cried if that boy resembling a lamppost wasn't standing there. I made sure I had enough gold for the entire year, but now I had nothing. I shouldn't have left it in my pocket, that was so stupid. If I found out who stole my gold I would do something... *evil* to them.

I sighed. Who was I kidding?

"I'm sorry I woke you," said the boy, he seemed to think he was the one who'd upset me.

"No it's not you, it's me. I've lost all my gold."

"Oh... bummer. Well I haven't got any money here either if it makes ya feel any better... me Dad couldn't get to the exchange place. I am from the normal world, I mean, I am from York, in England, in the other world..." he pointed. "Where are you from?"

I eyed him up, he was a nervous sort of lad who tried not to make eye contact. He had a big leather suitcase with wheels on it. The train jumped and shuddered and I nearly fell and smashed my face into the perplex glass window, but luckily I caught the seat just in time.

"I am from Happendance, the fourth Magical Kingdom... I'm Avis, Avis Blackthorn." It was safe to tell him my name, he was an Outsider. I stuck my hand out to shake, something my family would never do.

"Robin, Robin Wilson..." he said as we shook.

If I told most people my name, especially the second name, they would either run a mile or tell me what an evil family I had. But this kid Robin was from the Outside and, well, he hadn't a clue. Which meant, I had probably just made my first friend."

TINA PARTINGTON

Birthday: 18th December
    Favourite food: Strawberries
    Height: 5"0
    Form: Hubris

TINA PARTINGTON IS A COMPLICATED CHARACTER. As well as being feisty, clever and determined, she is in equal measures stubborn, unpredictable and moody.

IT'S in first year that Avis first meets her, normally forms don't mix too much in first year, but the reason Avis and Tina started talking was because Ross made the embarrassing pictures appear on Avis jacket when he was trying to impress and make friends. Tina is very empathetic and nice, so she did the right thing and escorted Avis out of the Chamber.* But it was later on that Avis would find out that Tina had secrets, through a chance meeting in the middle of the night Avis found Tina sneaking around, she tried to hide but he found her.**

THIS SETS up the most devilish of quests — find and rescue Tina's long lost brother who had been killed by Malakai some eight years previously.

Its toward the end of the first year when Avis discovers a big family connection between the people he knows. His form tutor Magisteer Partington was Tina's father. The ghost Ernie that helped him and kept him company through those solitary months, was Tina's long lost brother.

> * "One of the Magisteers came over. I didn't hear what she said, but escorted me by the shoulders out of the Chamber. I stared at the ground so I didn't have to see any more laughing faces. I could still hear the laughing as the Chamber doors shut.
>
> "Are you ok?" she said. I felt so numb I honestly didn't know so I just nodded. She put a hand on my

shoulder as the images kept flashing. Hold on, this wasn't a Magisteer. I looked up and saw the most beautiful girl I've ever seen. My sad watery eyes met these big, brown, saucer shaped eyes that sparkled back at me. She had skin like golden sunshine and a perfect, symmetrical face full of freckles. Her hair, a silky, shiny brown, swished around behind her.

"I thought, y-you were a Magisteer..." I stammered.

She laughed. "'Fraid not," we stood there in silence, the picture of me in the bath flashed up again. "My name's Tina by the way. Tina P."

"Nice to meet you Tina. I'm er... Avis... Avis B," she laughed, she knew what my last name was really.

"You a new year too?" she said.

"Yeap."

"It's tough the first few weeks isn't it?"

"It is when you have an evil brother who's determined to make you look like a fool, and it's... so hard to make friends."

"Well you've made one," she grinned and these shining, bright white teeth dazzled my eyes, honestly was a walking model for Toad-Eye Toothpaste. "And, what I find used to work for me was, if you laugh with them, make a joke out of yourself, then they can't laugh *at* you, they have to laugh *with* you."

She was bloody right, you know. This angel had to just walked into my life and saved me. As I watched her walk off back to the Chamber, I half expected her to flap a pair of white angel wings as she waved goodbye."

** Then, as we turned out of the bathrooms I swear I thought I saw someone. Out of the corner of my eye, I saw someone dart behind a suit of armour.

"You're not dreaming again are you?" said Robin.

"No, I wasn't before... just down there. I'm sure I saw someone. Come on."

Robin protested but soon followed. I was sure I had seen a person dash behind a suit of armour to the right. We tip toed along the corridor. And then, I knew I was right because I could see them, illuminated by the fire bracket above.

"Hello?" I said quietly. "I know there's someone behind that armour."

"Go away," said the voice.

I looked at Robin who wanted to take it's advice, but I was curious.

"It's alright, we're not Magisteers or anything."

I heard the person sigh then step out. The gas lamp above illuminated the golden skinned, sparkling eyes and brilliant white teeth of, "Tina?"

"Avis?" she looked like she had been prepared to give me a mouthful of verbal abuse, but she completely softened when she saw me. "What are you doing here?"

"I could ask you the same," I said.

"Who's lanky?"

"That's Robin," I said, as Robin waved awkwardly.

"We just went to the toilets," said Robin. "Not together, well together but..." he stopped.

"Right," said Tina eyeing him suspiciously.

"So what are you doing out here, creeping around?" I said.

"None of your business," she said curtly, then sighed again. "Oh fine, look, you both better promise not to say a *word*!"

I swore, sealing my mouth. Tina looked all flustered, her brilliant white teeth glowing in the darkness, her eyes perpetually scanning the hallways all around us. "I was trying to get into this door. I have a skeleton key but it doesn't seem to be working."

"A what key?" said Robin.

"A skeleton key," she said impatiently, holding it out. Robin was fascinated, he said he'd never seen a key made out of bone before. "It's supposed to open any lock, but it won't," she said.

The door looked pretty plain to me. "What's in there?"

She flicked her hair back, she was wearing her pyjamas too. "Well... that's kind of a secret I'm not willing to divulge."

"What if someone catches you?" I said.

"I'll just pretend I'm sleepwalking," she said matter of factly. "I'm in my jim-jams already... I shouldn't be telling you this... Let's just say, someone close to me, whom isn't with us anymore left me a quest, a big quest..." She turned away and fiddled with the key. "He was my older brother, he went to this school a few years ago. But he died and no one knew why... and then I found this note in his room with my name on. I've been trying to figure it out from then on," she didn't say anything else and after a few goes of the door each, we gave up. We walked back to our dorm, at the entrance to our corridor she gave me a rib cracking hug.

"Promise you won't say anything?"

"I promise," she waved goodbye to Robin and went, back into the darkness towards her dorm.

Avis, Robin and Tina. The best of friends.

❧ 6 ❧

NEMESIS

In the second year, there are some subtle, but big changes. Avis thinks that when he returns from the summer holidays that he and Tina will continued where they left off — as great friends (or more). But that is not the case at all. Enter Jasper.

JASPER MAKES Avis incredibly jealous as Tina and he spark a great friendship and spend all their time together. Avis develops a deep loathing hatred for the evil git who stole his love away from him. Primarily this is what causes the majority of problems throughout his second year.

BUT THEIR LOVE is not as it seems. In the third year, Avis discovers a horrifying fact — Jasper and Tina's love was not real. Someone had put a love spell on them both. When Avis discovers who, it puzzles him to the extreme.

JASPER IS TALL, good looking, immensely clever and well liked. He is the star player for his form the Swillows Riptide team and finished first in the rankings for Gold Stars, out of the entire school, at the end of his second year. He was almost anonymous in first year, so much so that the Magisteers remarked in the staff room that they thought he was new to the school. But Avis knows why Jasper has such a remarkable rise in grades and popularity — Jasper confesses to him when they are trapped in a classroom up high in the school after defeating Malakai that the Channeller his dead father gave him has *powers*. It seems to give him knowledge and magical help.

Their rivalry goes to the extreme — at Tina's birthday party, this happens…

"I stood alone on the dance floor mimicking Simon's awful dance moves without him realising.

Then I felt something wet go right down my front. "*Whoops…*" said a voice. Jasper! I looked down. He'd poured an entire glass of blood orange juice down my front. "That's what happens to those who aren't invited," he spat. I quickly looked around, no one saw, everyone was dancing. "Nice shirt," he smiled.

"How dare you do that to me!" I cried, fury boiling over. Without thinking, I pushed him as hard as I could. He sprawled across the floor falling backwards into some fourth years who dropped their drinks everywhere.

"*WOAH!*" they cried as Jasper jumped up and lunged at me, pushing me to the floor.

I clenched my fist and quickly said: "*Pasanthedine!*" Jasper shot into the air away from me, as I jumped up quickly. Then he smiled, raising his hands, a black shot of smoke punched me hard in the gut.

"Ahh!" I toppled forwards into dancing feet, hugging my stomach. Anger and frustration boiled up inside me. I stood quickly, raising my right hand at his throat and yelled: "*Aperchino!*" red wind burst out of my arm like fire. A satisfied glow lit up inside me, as my skin tingled. I felt myself fall back into the ground with the force as the red wind zapped towards his face. A silvery shield spell erupted in front of him. The red wind bounced off. There was a sudden and colossal *BANG!* As it hit the huge mirror above the fireplace, shattering it into a million pieces. A chorus of screams echoed deafeningly. A white layer of mist shot across the heads of all — Ernie's hands outstretched, as the shards of sharp mirror bobbed up and down above the white mist, just over the top of everyone's heads. Hayden stopped the music. Silence fell as eyes moved around to Jasper and I, standing with our arms out at each other.

"WHAT ON EARTH DO YOU THINK YOU ARE DOING?" Jasper called. "I know you don't like me, but there's no reason to do that!"

"*Whaat?*" I said as people started to look round at me with horror struck faces. "You started it!"

Tina stormed forwards through the crowd, then grimaced, pained as she saw me lying soaking wet on the ground. "What do you think you're doing?"

"He poured drink all over me, then—" I said, but she just closed her eyes, too angry to even look at me.

"You tried to ruin *my* party, and I NEVER EVEN INVITED YOU!" there was a horrible silence.

I swallowed. "But... why not?" I managed in a small voice.

"Because I knew what would happen. Because of how nasty you've been to Jasper lately. Because you are jealous of him!'"

THERE IS a constant battle between Jasper and Avis throughout the second year and everyone knows its because Avis is jealous about him and Tina. Jasper becomes enemy number one in Avis's eyes, replacing David Starlight by far. Avis has a feeling that Jasper is up to no good, even though Robin tries to tell him it's the jealousy talking. But stubborn as ever, Avis sets out to find out.

He discovers that Jasper is also a seventh son. He has the

same pendant as Avis, with the mark of the seventh son on. Jasper's father gave it to him, and he thinks that it passes him knowledge because he has become exceptionally more clever than last year. He has been using the Heptagon room (a room up high in the school that has seven sides, and is hidden by magic) all year to talk to his dead father, who gives him advice. In the Heptagon room there is a table that allows one to speak to the dead, you must bewitch yourself — black eyes — before seeing the dead the other side of the table.

AT THE END of the second year Jasper saves Avis from Malakai who tries to kill them both. And it's Jasper that speaks up and saves Avis's place at Hailing Hall — before the Lily can exspell him.

7

ERNIE PARTINGTON

E rnie is Tina's older brother and Magisteer Partington's son as Avis finds out at the end of his first year. The first time Avis meets Ernie, he is a ghost! When Avis is hiding out in the clock tower, Ernie finds and helps him, bringing him food and much needed light (ghosts give off a bluish light). They build up a big bond over the time they share together, Avis confessing every thing to Ernie, whom he believes was just another of the Hailing Hall ghosts.

But it's when Tina is attacked by Malakai, Ernie flies around in a mad state — Avis runs after him to the Healers room. Ernie soon confesses that Tina is his sister. Before he died, he sent his sister, by way of a Destiny Charm, all his notes on his mission to find and bring back their mother who was killed by Malakai. But Ernie in this quest ended up dying near the end of his seventh year at Hailing Hall. He came back as a ghost because he felt guilty passing the quest onto Tina, and could not 'pass on' until this was resolved.

After the showdown with Malakai, Robin uses the Book of Names to resurrect Avis and Ernie back to their bodies — which surprises everyone!

AFTER THIS, its decided between them that Ernie will take the credit for defeating Malakai and they invent a story that is beneficial for all, including Avis who could not face his family with them knowing that he had defeated their beloved boss.

IT'S while Avis is in the clock tower that Robin and Tina pay him a visit and they perform a revealing spell upon the amulet that Avis is using that happens to be the young Malakai's to try and get some clues... this leads them to see some fascinating things to do with Ernie...

> "A week later I was sitting, quietly watching Tina, when a thought flashed through my mind. *Use the revealing Spell on the key*!
>
> I ran back to the clock tower, knocking for Robin on the way. He was in the Condors' dorm doing his homework with the others. Our lessons

were being covered by a ghost, who kept setting more and more homework. Some of the Condors looked away when I poked my head in, but Robin saw my worried face and raced out.

"What's going on?" he said.

"Revealing Spell... on the... key!" I just about managed to say. We climbed through the roof hatch into the clock tower. I pulled the key out and put it on the dusty wood floor.

"Sit down," I said, raising my hands just above it and catching my breath. "What's the Spell?" I said, my mind had gone blank.

"Er... Kerka-something..." said Robin.

"I remember!" I raised my hands again. "*Kerkalculevreo!*" The key lit up orange, and my head flew back as a dream like vision danced across our eyes...

Ernie Partington looked very alive as he crept along the corridors. Every so often he would dart inside an alcove, or behind a suit of armour. Some way along the corridor was Malakai, drifting silently along. Then, in a flash he vanished inside a door and was gone. Ernie, with deep bags under his eyes, straightened and went over to inspect the door. Gently, he rubbed the lock, golden light fizzed around his hands, but he grew frustrated - the door wouldn't open. He stepped back and drew a wad of parchment from his back pocket and made notes. He sighed and turned back with a swish of his long, grey robes.

Then, with a whizz of white light, we zapped forwards. Ernie was on the floating island with friends, they all had silly haircuts, and some had beards. Ernie checked his watch, made an excuse to leave and walked back along the drawbridge. He was popular, people waved and cooed to him as he passed. As he approached the main hall, he scanned behind him to make sure no one was around, then screwing up his face he began rubbing his head viciously with his hands. A new face, body and clothes began to appear in place of him. Now a small man stood with a pudgy pock marked face, black robes and a Magisteer's crest. Quickly he began to walk toward the Dungeons. The small man walked through the hallways unnoticed, obviously not an important man. Yet, one boy, who was leaning over the banister rail above, saw him and set towards him calling out.

"Sir... Sir!" called the boy, running down the stairway.

"Yes?" called Ernie in a squeaky voice that he wasn't used to, then coughed. "Yes, what is it?"

"It's me Sir, Arnold? Just wondering Sir, about the homework, what is it? I thought I could do it now."

Ernie, as the little man kept walking and Arnold kept pace. "You will know the same time as everyone else."

"Oh right..." Arnold frowned. "But you said earlier I must find you and ask."

"Yes," said Ernie, stopping and scratching his head, this was an unwanted distraction. "What were we studying earlier?" he said, as if trying to remember.

"The transformation of Biglobears and Faradays into Yerpold creatures."

"Ah yes," said Ernie. "Well, do me two passages on other Yerpold creatures and why it's important that we know."

Arnold frowned again. "Only two passages sir?" this was obviously not what he was used to and he smelt something fishy.

Sweat beads appeared on Ernie's forehead, he scanned the hallway where a dozen or so people were milling around. Slyly, Ernie raised his hand at Arnold and muttered something under his breath.

"I *see* Sir," said Arnold, who promptly ran off looking happy. Ernie smiled and carried on in the direction of the dungeons. That was close.

"But, no one has requested that key in years, I'm not sure I even have it. If I do, it will be rusted over..."

Ernie looked down at the man who was shorter even than he, whom had bags and bags of keys on chains around his waist. "I was assured you would have it by the Lily himself, but if you want me to go and tell him why you can't do your job then..."

"No! No... I can find it, all I mean is... are you sure it's *that* door he wants the key for?" the small, dirty man looked sideways at Ernie with yellowing eyes. The dungeon was dank, mouldy and echoed with the sound of scuttling creatures, Ernie didn't feel altogether comfortable. The man reached down and slid a key off a chain, and handed it to Ernie, who nodded and turned back.

"The next flash and Ernie was alone at a desk. Dim orange embers glowed throughout the room. There was snoring behind him, as the other boys in the room slept. Ernie had his head in his hands, pouring over notes. He collected the sheets together, set a note down and wrote *Tina,* on the top, folded it, tapped it three times and with a poof of smoke, it vanished. Then he did the same with a thick bundle of notes.

Finally, he pulled out a key and a book. With his head bowed over the page and right hand poised over they key, he recited the instructions. Fiery green light outlined the contours of another key next to the existing one. He placed the original inside a small green box with red ribbon. He sealed the box and began to read another passage. The box jolted and span on his desk, then shrank and popped, disappearing altogether. Ernie sat back in his chair and sighed, brushing his long hair back. He took the copied key, which was loosely transparent.

"Haven't got long..." he muttered, twisting it round in his hands. Then, putting his grey robes on, looked around the room as if for the last time. With a swish, he left. Ernie walked purposefully, grey robe flapping behind, not making much attempts at quieting his footsteps. He took the key out of his pocket and unlocked the door with a loud clunk and stood back. The door creaked. Ernie brushed his hair back, and steeled himself, before stepping into darkness.

Ernie crept down through darkness. The next second he stood, facing a large man dressed all in black, face long and skeletal with blue glowing eyes that came to rest on Ernie, who raised his hands quickly. Red, green and gold flashes scorched the air. Malakai flapped and the light burst in a shard of sparks. The two foes faced each other. With a long skeletal hand Malakai pinned Ernie to the floor. A very large book with a brown cover, older than time itself, stood on a gold mantle."

"How dare you! Coming here and interfering in *my* business!" Malakai cried.

Ernie looked charged, he whispered something and vanished, like a mirage. The next moment he was behind Malakai. "*Flutteryout!*" he cried.

Malakai flew into the opposite wall. Ernie grabbed the book, which fizzed and made horrible cracking noises. Malakai roared.

"Give that back! Don't you dare!" A whistling lit the air. Ernie stood terrified, unable to move. The next moment he was bound by thick red snaking, chains. Malakai took the book and placed it back on the mantle carefully. Ernie struggled against the expanding chains.

"You will never get away with what you're doing. I will make sure of it! I know your plans. I won't stop until your gone!" said Ernie before a red chain bound his mouth.

Malachi chuckled. "Oh please... I've heard it all before."

Another flash of white light and Ernie stood motionless, bound in red chains, at the top of the tallest tower in the school. High pitched wind whistled around the open top. Malakai came to stand and look down at the drop into abyss. "Any last words?"

The chain around Ernie's mouth disappeared. Ernie's eyes were large, but he didn't look like a man about to die.

"You know nothing! There are thousands of other people ready to take my place. The plans I have this year are already making their way to the right people. I followed you the whole year and you haven't spotted me. You think you're powerful, you think your special, you think your power gives you a right to rule! It doesn't. You're weak, your lust for power comes from a loss of love. And I pity you."

Malakai's blue eyes dimmed, and his head tilted to the side. With a lazy flick of his finger, the red chains fell off. "Maybe, but you're the one whose about to die..."

"I'm not afraid..." Ernie smiled as wind whipped his hair and clothes.

Malakai huffed and swiped the air. Ernie slid across the floor. He didn't struggle. He just kept his gaze with Malakai and in silence, slid off the tower."

8

MALAKAI

"He is the most evil high master Sorcerer these Seven Kingdoms have ever seen. He's killed more people than a Wolfraptor (a huge, flying, killer wolf). In fact, if a Wolfraptor came face to face with Malakai, it would probably scream like a girl and fly away (no offence to any girls). My parents are totally and utterly in love with him and think he does tiny golden nugget poo's. They are always talking about him.

I've only ever seen him once and had nightmares ever since. He wears this dark black hood like Death and carries this huge wooden staff and his hands... his hands are like black charred skeletons hands, all bony and disfigured. He even spoke to me once. He asked me, in his deep rasping voice like splintering wood if I, like the rest of family, would be coming to work for him when I left school. I didn't say anything."

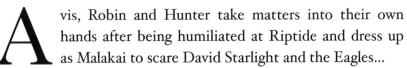

A vis, Robin and Hunter take matters into their own hands after being humiliated at Riptide and dress up as Malakai to scare David Starlight and the Eagles...

"Robin climbed on top of Hunter's shoulders and I threw the huge grey sheet over them. I passed Robin the armour mask, the shiny blue eyes and the long skeletal claws. Together, we said the Spells that transformed the collection of objects into a terrifying effigy. Small horns poked out of the armour head, which now looked like a long skull. The blue robe patches now shined bright beneath the skulled face. The long grey sheets, now a seamless black cape covering them in shadow. And the long skeletal, charred hands needed no Spellwork. The person who now stood over me was not Robin and Hunter... it was Malakai."

Avis standing with the fake Malakai (Robin and Hunter with a big cloak on).

THE NEWSPAPER, the Herrald is always reporting on Malakai and what he is up to...

> *"Today, we bring you the startling revelation that the
> mass murderer and high Sorcerer known as Malakai,
> is back! — Hundreds of witnesses last night claimed
> that they saw the mysterious man, in various towns
> across the Seven Magical Kingdoms. This follows a
> spate of murders in the same areas. It seems his rise
> back to power has been rapid. No one knows where
> he was hiding all this time or what he was doing, but
> we are sure Ernie Partington, the teenager who
> claimed to have defeated Malakai will be answering
> a lot more questions very soon. Last April it was
> reported that Malakai was defeated—some
> commentators said even then, that you cannot
> suppress a force such as his. "It will take a lot more
> than whatever Ernie Partington, a teenager, did, to
> keep Malakai from returning..." said Grenville
> Summerville, WMP for Defence for the Magical
> Council. "Defeating someone is not the same as
> ending someone." Witnesses have released the photo's
> that they bravely took of the returned Malakai."*

AVIS IS ASKED to go and see the Lily. This meeting is what leads
Avis to discover that he has the very same amulet as Malakai,
which ultimately allows Avis to say Malakai's true name and
defeat him. You see, the Lily shows Avis a picture of the young
Malakai at school — on his wrist is the exact same amulet chan-
naller that Avis got from lost property!

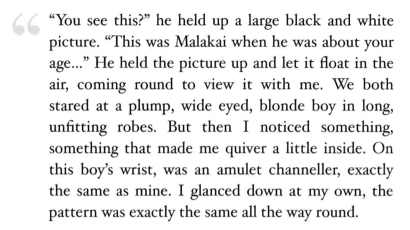

"You see this?" he held up a large black and white picture. "This was Malakai when he was about your age..." He held the picture up and let it float in the air, coming round to view it with me. We both stared at a plump, wide eyed, blonde boy in long, unfitting robes. But then I noticed something, something that made me quiver a little inside. On this boy's wrist, was an amulet channeller, exactly the same as mine. I glanced down at my own, the pattern was exactly the same all the way round.

AVIS, somehow manages to formulate a plan to topple Malakai. He doesn't know if it will work — he only knows that to save Tina from dying, then he must act and do something. So while everyone is at Riptide, Avis sneaks away and goes to find him. In the secret room in Hailing Hall, down a long flight of stairs under a dark passage, Malakai is working, using the Book of Names.

In his second year at Hailing Hall, Malakai has had his

powers reduced, but more so; he has reduced in size and stature, now resembling a small grubby leprechaun. Malakai is consumed with thoughts of revenge as he tries to conserve his powers and get them back. It's mid-way through the second year when strange accidents start to occur; accidents surround Avis as things seemingly try and kill him. But they are not coincidences, it's Malakai attempting to get his revenge.

- Accident 1: while building the Riptide Stadium, a huge rafter swings round at Avis, atop a scaffolding and knocks him off.
- Accident 2: a statue in the boys Riptide changing rooms dislodges and falls towards them.
- Accident 3: an ember from the fire jumps into Avis's bed and sets it on fire while something else holds onto his legs.
- Accident 4: Dawn eats a pudding intended for Avis and starts to choke.
- Accident 5: a chandelier in the bathrooms falls at him and nearly kills him.

Avis in the bathrooms when the taps suddenly explode and the chandelier falls on him.

9

THE SEVEN MAGICAL KINGDOMS

HAPPENDANCE

Is the nicest kingdom, even though Avis would tell you otherwise. Its sunny in summer, cold but not freezing in winter and has a brilliant spring. It's a bit like the British Isles in terms of weather. Happendance is covered in forest and as Avis points out, is populated with many 'stupid, annoying, fairytale creatures' — things like Leprechauns, Gnomes, Pig-people, as well as witches, enchanted animals, wise-men and a whole host of everything in between, but they are at least peaceful.

MANY A PERSON from the Outside has fallen through a hole in a tree in their world only to find themselves tumbling head first into the magical world too, and returned to their world and penned the tale.

Leprechauns dancing in a Happendance forest.

FARKINGHAM

Is a black dust bowl and void and empty of life. The trees are black and dead, and the atmosphere is creepy. You won't last long, if you find yourself in Farkingham alone. Wizards still live there, for the apparent peace, as they can sustain themselves with their magic.

THE REASON IS became a black dustbowl, was due to, they think, a magical war and a curse being put on the Kingdom by a thousand demons. And now, oddly, the only things that really live there, are demons. Or the lost dead. You can see them too, if you hang around long enough, peering at you through the trees with their red eyes.

GOLANDRIA

Is a large kingdom that grew into existence when Russian and eastern european wizards started to wake up to their innate talents and needed a place to live in peace away from persecution. The magical kingdom welcomed them warmly, with a similar environment to what they were used to. It's bitterly cold in winter, and not much better in summer. But the people are hard, and used to it.

GOLANDRIA IS A VERY GOTHIC KINGDOM, the people like tall houses that resemble a melted waxwork, glooping and drooping upwards with sharp bits and gargoyles. It's a strange taste which is oddly beautiful in it's own way.

LUNDORIA

Is a strange kingdom and very large with vast wild-grass plains, almost orange ground and huge green lakes.

THE POPULATION IS NOT LARGE, and it only has one big city; Nodnol, which is one of the most important cities in the Seven Magical Kingdoms and houses many important government buildings, including the Lundorian monarchy and a large wizarding gold trading island.

THERE IS TALK, a myth, that this city is twinned magically with London, from the outside — and they magically mirror each other.

GILLIGAN

Is a charming, sleepy Kingdom. It could be compared to Switzerland in looks and politics. The towns sit in valleys around the mountainous, beautiful surroundings. They get involved with the politics of the magical kingdoms as less as possible, preferring to keep to themselves.

MANY A FAMOUS WIZARD have come from Gilligan, but all leave Gilligan to make it.

SLACKERDOWN

Is the arctic of the magical lands. It's permanently snowy, icy, and treacherous in most areas. There are few towns and cities to the south of Slackerdown that are moderately liveable. But the north is a no-go area, unless you have some seriously good magic to help. Anyway, there is nothing there.

THE SLACKERDOWN FOLK ARE HARD, but lazy folk who stick to their Inns and drink a lot.

MODAFAFA

Could be attributed to be the spiritual-magical home of Africa. They are very similar in lots of ways: it's very hot, it has vast plains of lush wildlife, jungles and rivers.

It's also the home of the *Fafazards* a very ancient tribe of wise ones, who seek to better humanity by helping the Earth.

OTHER IMPORTANT PLACES

DODECATRON

Mentioned by Magisteer Stracker in Avis' second year — it's a big wizarding city where the magical government sits, on the borders of Happendance and Golandria, in what could be said was the centre of the wizarding world.

GNIPPOH'S, THE SHOPPING TOWN.

The shopping town of Gnippoh's is infamous in wizarding circles. It's not the only shopping place, but it's known as the shopping town. The whole town is just shops. Embedded in the heart of Southern Happendance, it receives thousands of eager shoppers daily, to get their magical goods.

SOME SHOPS FROM GNIPPOH'S MENTIONED IN THE BOOK:

RUBENS ROBES

A clothes shop selling exclusively robes for your magical school (as there is more than just Hailing Hall). Ever-changing robes are what the pupils at Hailing Hall wear, they change colour depending on what year you are in. If you pay more, you can also get some that change size depending on how much you grow (or how much weight you put on). They also sell trousers that do the same, very handy, especially with those buffet dinners.

SORDINA'S SWEET EMPORIUM.

Got a sweet tooth? Come to Sordina's, it's the only place to get your hands on Squirming Snake Jellies, Exploding Sugar Eggs, Love-potion-laced lollipops (with a temporary effect of course), Sherbert Shandy's (popular because they had a bit of beer in them).

THE PERCEVIUS DENN INN

So named after the Percevius spell, this Inn has some notoriety for being a rough pub, attracting unsavoury characters. At the start of the second year at Hailing Hall in the summer holidays, Avis found himself in Gnippoh's, so took residency in one of the rooms, which was small and dirty, but cheap and it had views across Gnippoh's town square.

— MOST PUBS ARE NAMED after a spell or charm. Take the *Slackerdown Sevhurton Inn* for example, or *Gofandeious on the Green*, or even *The King's Kerchaveleo*.

THE HAPPENDANCE CARNIVAL

In their second year at Hailing Hall, pupils are taken on a school trip to the Happendance Carnival. It's a very big organised event spread out across huge fields. You can buy magical items from the miles and miles of stalls selling everything from magical animals to antique artefacts. You could get something tasty to eat from a stall, or restaurant. A Sherbet Shandy from the numerous pubs and Inns. You could watch a presentation in the evening with famous wizards, witches and speakers on a host of differing issues. For example, you could poke your head into one tent and watch: *"Rupert Greers Hypno-Magical Presentation"* — Where he demonstrates the magical art of hypnotising and commanding his foes to do what he wants. Avis knows only too well, his Father is a master at making you do things you don't want to with his hypnotic voice. Or you could terrify yourself by going to watch someone raise and capture a demon, on stage and hold it in a special glass. Or, if you were there when Avis was, you would have got to see Jack Hummingbird hold a small presentation demonstrating Illusions, and how to create them.

THE OUTSIDE:

 "As most of you reading this will probably be from the Non-Magical lands, or *The Outside*, as we call it, I suppose I had better explain: we, Wizards, live in a similar dimension to you, but separate and kind of invisible..."

GROWING UP, Avis was always told terrible things about the Outside. How dangerous it was and the things they would do to someone like him, a wizard. It scared him silly and he never thought much more of it. The wizarding news on TV was no better, it constantly went on about some bad things that were happening on the Outside, war mostly, so Avis vowed that he should never go there. When he met Robin, however, they shared their knowledge of their respective homes — Avis telling Robin about the intricacies of the wizarding world, and Robin telling Avis that the Outside was not scary at all.

❧ 10 ❧

MAGISTEERS

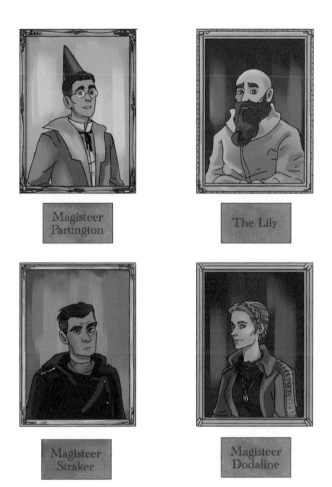

Magisteer
Partington

The Lily

Magisteer
Straker

Magisteer
Dodaline

MAGISTEER (HENRY ALBERT) PARTINGTON

Has the face of an owl, all pointed and expectant. He wears small round spectacles and a tall triangular hat, that used to be fashionable on a wizard, but Partington insists on still wearing his. It used to have stars and moons on it, but they have since faded.

HE WAS BORN A HAPPENDANCIAN. I can't tell you what year he was born, as they have a different system for counting the years than we do. But he is in his early fifties.

THIS IS what we know about Magisteer Partington: he joined Hailing Hall twenty years ago, teaching first years, as he has a soft manner, and many of the people starting in their first year are very tentative, so this helps settle them in. The previous first year tutor was a very brash man, causing half the first years to quit after three weeks.

HIS WIFE MARCELA, died some ten years ago in mysterious circumstances. She worked for the magical council and was an Mediator, which meant she oversaw negotiations between different races, to make sure they were all happy with the deal and no one is being scammed. It's a hard, demanding job.

HIS SON ERNIE was killed by Malakai in his last year at school. He would have been a broken man, if it were not for his daughter Tina. But at the end of Avis's first year at school, he and Robin help to resurrect Ernie to his body using the Book of Names and Partington is ecstatic.

MAGISTEER (UNKNOWN FIRST NAME) STRAKER

Magisteer Straker always wears grey, he does not own anything else — no one quite knows why he only wears grey. He is regarded very highly at Hailing Hall as one of the best Magisteers they have.

IN FIRST YEAR, he and Avis do not get on. Straker likes the Blackthorns, they are good competent wizards, but is disappointed to see that Avis had not inherited any of their talents.

HOWEVER, in the second year when Straker is charged with escorting Avis around the school to hunt out the Djinn, they get to know each other and Straker changes his mind — especially when he suspects that Avis may have saved his life, when the *Death Corridor* collapses.

HE TOO USED to be a Mediator before taking up a more relaxing role as a Magisteer at Hailing Hall. He was born a Golandrian, but moved around a lot as a child, as his Father was a serial law-breaker, finally settling in Farkingham when he was ten. He attended Farkingham Mystery School where he was teased about being poor. But grew up to be one of the most effective wizards in all of Farkingham.

MAGISTEER (GRACE BOVEY) DODALINE

She has been at Hailing Hall longer than anyone, she started when was in her twenties and is now in her late fifties.

DODALINE IS the Magisteer that is the first to greet the new first years, waiting on the grass courtyard before entering Hailing Hall. She is, for a lot of them, the first glimpse of magic they will have seen.

SHE TEACHES CHARMS — how to charm something to your will. It's an important lesson they must take in their fourth year.

THE LILY

The term 'Lily' simply refers to the fact that you have reached a certain level (Lv. 34) of *light magic* that means you have achieved the *pure of heart* status that makes one become magically robed in white, in a ceremonial occasion with many people watching on.

THE LILY (real name not known: it is hidden by magic when one becomes a Lily and is terrifically hard to uncover again), became the Headmaster of Hailing Hall seven years before Avis started, when the previous Headmistress vanished.

MAGISTEER (UNKNOWN) SIMONE

Is known as the firebrand at Hailing Hall — she takes no pris-oners whatsoever. If she had it her way, she would be practicing magical booby traps as punishment for bad behaviour "just like the good old days!" But Avis, Robin and Hunter were on the end of her dark punishments in second year, when they broke into her private quarters and had a look around for clues, as they thought she was helping Malakai, but then they triggered a trap and a huge spiked boulder came of the wall and they had to run for their lives! That's what starts to cause all the problems with Avis's jumper, when it gets spiked and starts going weird and tries to kill him!

SHE TEACHES Physical and Mental Training, a class which would
be fine if she was not teaching it. In their second year when
they start the class, in the first lesson they are run so ragged
with sprints, push ups and press ups that most of them are
violently sick. Magisteer Simone just calls them 'worms' and
walks out.

MAGISTEER (RALPH EDWARD FRANCIS) COMMONSIDE

A bit of a joke of a teacher at Hailing Hall — he is regarded as
being slightly mad, completely obsessed with numbers and his

lessons in which he teaches Numerology. He insists on holding his classes in a broom cupboard because it's numbered III.

MAGISTEER (JULIE ANNE) UNDERWOOD

Is the Riptide referee and Riptide tutor for the Hailing Hall school team. She also takes Physical and Mental Training when Magisteer Simone is away. Underwood is a tough teacher and very good referee. She was a professional player herself, with the 'Leaping Leprechaun Athletic' for almost twelve years scoring over 443 goals and achieving a team record as captain of 73 Libero-Manus's.

MAGISTEER (ERIC) YEARLOVE

Avis, Robin and the Condors get taught by Magisteer Yearlove in second year in a mixed class with Hubris and the Swillows (Tina and Jasper).

HE IS KIND, clever and understanding teacher who has a passion for his classes; Spell-craft. Previous to being a teacher, he wrote new spells for the Magical Council that were released to the public.

HE IS tall and good looking with a thick black beard, quite unfashionable these days, but that doesn't bother him.

MAGISTEER (ARTHUR OSCAR) MALLARD

Is a flouncy, loud and attention-seeking person who teaches Drama. You might think; what need do wizards have for drama and acting? And its a fair ask. Well, it's noted that some of the best and most distinguished wizards were fantastic actors — to be able to hide ones intentions before spelling is vitally important, especially in a duel. But also, acting classes help them to grow their emotional and playful sides. Most lessons are in stuffy classrooms and involve learning lots of complicated words and meanings. Actors and plays are held in high esteem, even in the wizarding world, because to command the attention of an audience is a sign of leadership.

MALLARD CLAIMS to be a former actor in several famous plays but is now retired. But some have their doubts as to the validity of his claims.

MAGISTEER (JACOB JUNIPER) WASP

He is likened to a cherub in a suit, with soft blonde curly hair and an exuberant personality. If you ask him about his past during a lesson, he will regail you with awesome stories completely forgetting the lesson.

He teaches them Astro-magic, which is the study of magical astrology.

MAGISTEER (HAROLD KAZIER) BLACKTHORN

Avis's eldest brother Harold starts at the school in Avis's second year, much to his horror. Avis thinks that this must be to keep an eye on him, seeing as his other brother Ross left last year. Harold takes Infusions, which he is very proficient at, in fact he could probably teach most of the lessons at Hailing Hall. That's what makes Avis suspicious — the fact that Harold could be doing anything, and yet he chooses to work at Hailing Hall.

II

ROBES AND TIES

THE COLOURS OF ROBES AND TIES AND THEIR MEANINGS

TIES

The colour of ones tie refers to the level of ones magic. First years ties will be bright turquoise (complete beginners — Lvl. 1) but as they learn, grow and progress, their ties naturally change colour reflecting the level that they are now on. The first couple of years at school take a long time to progress through the levels, but when they have the momentum, they will rocket through them and should expect to leave Hailing Hall having completed all 33 levels of the first section.

THERE ARE three *sections* of magic levels. The first section is called Unicus, the second is Umbilicus and the last is Extimum.

THE FIRST TWO have 33 levels in them. The last has 34. Once you get to that level and have trained exclusively in white/light magic you become a Lily (note: this is extremely hard and rare to achieve) as to learn some black/dark magic is needed in most cases.

AT THE END of the seventh year, you will take the P.W.W Exam, which stands for *Professional Working Wizard* — to be classed as a professional wizard and to be able to work as one, you must pass this exam. Anyone who doesn't is not qualified to work as a wizard anywhere in the Seven Magical Kingdoms.

COLOUR OF TIE TO LEVEL OF MAGIC:

- Level 1 - Turquoise
- Level 2 - Maroon
- Level 3 - Cream
- Level 4 - Brown
- Level 5 - Navy
- Level 6 - Green
- Level 7 - Yellow

AS YOU PROGRESS through higher levels, the colours must take on specific shades, for instance, level 23 is *duck egg blue*, level 27 is *fuchsia*, and level 32 is silver. There are only so many colours, but

100 levels of magic and so must resort to specific shades. However, it's not likely that anyone in school will achieve levels past section Unicus. To avoid confusion, just inside the flap of the tie your level of magic will be written.

THE TIE WAS INVENTED by Michaela Cernovich and Anne Knowles, both Magisteers at Hailing Hall, who spoke at length in the staff room one day about how difficult it was to see who was struggling and who was excelling in their work. And so they devised a system when a tie, worn around the neck could read the aura of the wizard and relay back to the tie their magical knowledge and thus forming a colour.

IT WAS LATER FITTED with anti-tamper magic to stop people from charming their ties to be a different colour that would allow them on a school trip, or to pass a specific exam.

ROBES

The robes at Hailing Hall are everchanging robes — this is not usual, other schools like Farkingham mystery school just use black robes with the school crest on. But the way Hailing Hall is set up with a Chamber where forms could mix, it needed a system where the Magisteers could easily identify the years.

EVERCHANGING ROBES CANNOT BE FOOLED, they know what year you are in. If someone in the seventh year put your robe on, it would turn green.

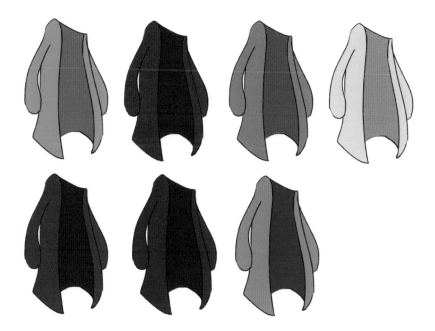

- 1st year — Turquoise
- 2nd year — Red
- 3rd year — Orange
- 4th year —Yellow
- 5th year — Purple
- 6th year — Navy
- 7th year — Green

In his first year at school, Avis's parents forget to take him shopping so he has hardly anything that was on the list of things to bring. So, he has to follow the ghost Impkus, down into the dungeons to the lost property room and find some...

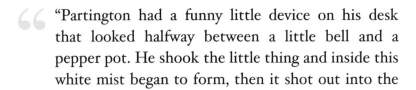 "Partington had a funny little device on his desk that looked halfway between a little bell and a pepper pot. He shook the little thing and inside this white mist began to form, then it shot out into the

room. This transparent man, all haughty and dead looking, said impatiently.

"Yeaass?"

"Impkus, can you take Avis here to lost property and see if we can find him some Ever-changing robes, tie, and channeller?"

Impkus, the ghost, nodded slowly then floated off through the door. Partington indicated for me to follow. I sighed, glad of a reason to leave the room and had to run to keep up with the ghost who sailed off down the winding staircase. I followed as best I could as he darted into a main corridor, then straight through a large tapestry. I went under it and followed the glowing white light down three flights of stairs. It was cold down here.

"These are the dungeons..." said Impkus. "Don't make a habit of coming down here too often, unless you want to end up like me."

I didn't know what he meant, it was dark and damp but I couldn't see any danger or way of being murdered.

He zapped through a big metal door to the left, then pushed it open for me form the inside. The lost property room was bigger than I thought and filled to the brim with stuff piled up as high as the eye could see. The smell was an overpowering aroma of centuries old dust, something dead and rotten, mixed with a fifty year old broken bottle of Butterfly perfume.

"So you need some Ever-changing robes?" said Impkus chucking an enormous cardboard box to the ground in front of me. I had a short coughing fit as the plumes of dust went up my nose. Inside the box was a mass of tangled silky black ever-changing robes. He made me search through them and boy they stank! I found a few that fitted ok, but they just smelt so bad I had to put them back. Eventually I picked out the only one that didn't smell of mouldy feet and put it on. It was miles too big and the bottom trailed on the floor behind me, but it didn't smell.

"This one will do," I said as the colours changed. The black faded into this horrible bright turquoise just like the carpet in our dorm room.

"Here's a tie," said Impkus, handing me this thing that looked like a chewed up and dead snakeskin. He noticed my hesitation and huffed. "A tie's a tie's a tie." I took it and stuffed it in my robe's pocket, glancing around to see if there were any others I could quickly take, but there were none in sight. There were lots of old rusty cauldrons, dented kettles and things floating in jars but no spare ties."

IN THEIR SECOND YEAR, Avis bumps into Robin and Tina in Gnippoh's, so they go shopping. Now that Avis has some gold, he thinks he may as well spend some on new clothes! He can finally get rid of the old, second-hand robes and get himself some new ones. So they enter...

"RUBEN'S ROBES"

 There were more robes in this shops than I had ever seen in my life. "This is the place to get them," [said Tina.] You could do with some more as well Robin, I seem to remember you grew out of last years."

Robin grimaced.

"Welcome to Ruben's Robes!" called an excitable man coming around his desk. He had a pencil behind his ear and a big bushy moustache. "Right... Hailing Hall?" he said looking at me.

"Yes Sir," I said and he nodded, his eyes scanning me all over before narrowing as he twisted his moustache, deep in thought. A notebook and pencil jumped into his hand as he began to write what I presumed to be measurements. After a few flicks through all the rails in the shop he stopped.

"Aha! Here we are. Just the right sized everchanging robe... you'll be a first year will you?"

"No! Second," I said a little sourly.

"Second, right, well this should do you," he handed me a long, brilliant robe. It felt heavy and as I touched it, it turned bright blood red.

"Wow," said Robin just behind me.

I was so glad I now actually had robes that would fit me properly, I wouldn't look like a leprechaun anymore! Robin was measured and bought some robes that extended if, or as, he grew. Once we had our new robes wrapped, bagged and paid for, we moved on together and shopped.

12

LESSONS

Magical lessons, which we have touched on briefly in the Magisteers section, are very different to lessons in your world. A magic school must teach a wizard to function with every type of magic known.

AVIS WENT to a magical theory school before attenting Hailing Hall, which involved no practical magic at all. So, when he and the Outsiders start at Hailing Hall, they are all on an equal footing.

THEY CAN, after Hailing Hall, go to a University — there are a few around the Seven Magical Kingdoms to choose from and to study one particular craft in depth and enter the second section of magic, so deeply investing oneself in a particular subject.

A magical classroom. What's different about this compared to your school classroom?

SPELL-CRAFT

This lesson, taught by Magisteer Yearlove, teaches one how to use a spell properly. But more than just being able to spell properly, spell-craft is about how you fuse together two spells.

LET'S say you want to freeze a Sprat but not harm it. Individually, a freeze spell will most likely kill it. So, you need to fuse Sevhurton with a protection spell, thus it will encase the Sprat in ice, but not harm it. The protection spell could be: *Helipus*, when you combine the two together they work as one. This is simplistic example, as it gets more complicated, depending on what kind of effect you want to cause. Let's use the example of a piano — you can only play certain keys on certain chords, if you play a key that doesn't go well with a chord it will sound wrong.

In the same way, every spell has other spells that it can and cannot go with.

MAGISTEER YEARLOVE'S CLASSROOM:

Magisteers Yearlove's room was magnificent. It looked like a cathedral. Golden beams stretched from ceiling to floor propping up a colossally high pitched roof. Stone arches held up a second floor, which ran around the outside of the room. All around the outside, under the stone archways that went all the way around the room, had piles of stuff inside. Stuffed into the shadows were piles of old battered books, silvery instruments and old paintings. The ceiling was decorated with the most elaborate magical paintings of the scenes of the magical war and the Jermain and Shaun-John magical revolution. The images were so cool, popping out of the ceiling whenever you looked at them — like real cool magical art should be — not like those boring paintings in the corridors. Colour streamed in through the stain glass windows, casting a rainbow of light across the white stone floor. Stairs floated in mid air at the far end of the room, in a spiral with no hand rails — right to the very top of the ceiling. It was so magical and awe inspiring... at the very end of the room was a miniature version of Hailing Hall. A life-size model of the entire school complete with Riptide pitch, floating garden and grounds — and it was moving! The trees swayed, the statues moved and the sun beat down upon it. The top of the centre spire of

the model was complete with a blue glass dome —
where we had our lesson with Magisteer Wasp.

NUMEROLOGY

Taken by Magisteer Commonside it focuses on the magic of
numbers — regarded as some as bit of a cop-out of a lessons and
a lesser-lesson, made no better by the boring teacher, it's not
held in high regard at Hailing Hall.

IN FACT the magic stems from Ancient Egyptian wizards, who
used magic squares placed in a certain position to cause the
warranted effect; grow crops, induce rainfall, better fertility.

PHYSICAL AND MENTAL TRAINING

You might be thinking 'what does running and fitness have to do
with being a wizard?' Well... to be a good wizard, you must be fit.
It takes a huge amount of effort and strength to do magic, to
cast a spell, to conjure a charm, to enchant a tree or stir an infu-
sion for 36 hours straight. Every spell or piece of magic that you
set into motion (a spoon stirring your tea) takes a portion of
your energy as if you were stirring the tea yourself. It's just more
convenient to have magic do it for you while you get on with
something else.

There is always a trade off with anything and magic is no
different. But also, to be a wizard you must have a clear head,
functioning brain and focused concentration on your task —
excersize helps with this, but another part of the lessons, which
they will take later on, will include learning to align their concentration into a laser-like focus on one thing and not allowing
anything to distract them. You see, our minds are quite clumsy

and without training you will have clumsy wizards. No one wants that, especially with magic.

ASTROMAGIC

Classes are taken at the tallest part of Hailing Hall in a circular observatory with a domed roof which opens to reveal the night sky. In their fifth year they take midnight lessons in AstroMagic to better see and understand the night sky.

AstroMagic is different from Astrology in that it focuses mainly on the magical side of Astrology, although their first few years are studying basic Astrology to back up their later knowledge in AstroMagic.

Magisteer Wasp will tell any naysayers that AstroMagic is a "warranted, subtle and powerful magic, just look what happens every full moon! Crime goes through the roof." The moon, he says, has an effect upon Earth. In the way that the moon effects earths water; the tides of the sea, so, in the same way, it will effect humans and wizards who are roughly the same quantity of water as the Earth — 80%.

Learning AstroMagic is a painful, dull process, but once learnt can be exceptionally helpful. One wizard; Iain McGregor (*deceased*) says he owed his career to it. Before learning Astro-Magic he was a simple farm hard, living on a pittance, but at night he would stare at the night sky, studying it from a book he borrowed from a travelling library *The Magic of the Stars & Planets, by Niko Gravel.* Iain soon learnt what spells and magic would work better at what times; what months would be best for particular infusions, and what years what be best for bold actions. Armed with this new knowledge, he set out, leaving the farm on a mission to be remembered. He sure was remembered, remembered as being one of the best Magical Prime Ministers of the SMK's (Seven Magical Kingdoms) of all time. This was due, in his own words, no doubt to the fact that he assimilated Astro-Magic into his own magic, using his own compendium of spells, charms, infusions, hexes and enchantments and what should/could be used when.

INFUSIONS

Avis studies Infusions in his second year at Hailing Hall, not realising that Harold, his brother is his new teacher. Infusions is a powerful, dangerous and beautiful subject. It's liquid alchemy. You take certain liquids and combine them, creating a combination of ingredients that together, make a powerful effect. Infusions or Potions is a long established lesson, much like the long established tradition that it is in the wizarding world. Used for hundreds, maybe even thousands of years, originally as medicine, but upon experimentation, wizards realised that these potions could do more than just heal. A lot more. They could brew good fortune, capture happiness, smell death.

IT'S A COMPLICATED LESSON, but a rewarding one — the ample Infuser can make a good fortune selling his wares.

AN ACCIDENT IN SPELL-CRAFT

It's in these lessons, during his second year with Magisteer Yearlove that a strange incident occurs to Avis...

"As we were watching Jake and Hunter nervously read aloud their charm, our flower which was dancing just within my vision began to do something *strange*. It started to grow. It was as if something else had taken over it. In one flash it had reached the ceiling.

"Sir! SIR!" we cried.

Yearlove turned frowning, before jumping backwards. "Goodness gracious me! What on earth could have done tha—" Yearlove stopped. We all stopped, open mouthed as the flower changed dramatically. The light outside the windows suddenly vanished as we were plunged into darkness, the flower widened, stalk thickening. The pot burst as long snaking roots dived into the cracks of the floor. Then all at once, it dived.

"AHH!" Screamed the class falling back, apart from me... snaking up my body were long, green tentacled vines. Thick and waxy, they encircled my body from feet to chest, winding slowly up towards my head. I didn't even have time to think, it was all happening so quickly. What was happening? Yearlove had backed the class away and was gazing up at me, suspended in mid air. I was *so* high, my stomach twisted as I spun like a fly in a spiders web. I tried to double tap my feet, but they were bound so tightly I was all but paralysed, the breath slowly being squeezed out of me.

Raising both arms, Yearlove shouted: "*Relovotessellaregrassus!*" all in one go. There was a flash of brightest orange, as flames suddenly speared the thick snaking body of the flower. Leaves burned, as it let out a screeching cry, before releasing me and wilting away. Burning to ash as it fell to the floor in a clump of smouldering green debris. I hit the pile of green ash and lay panting, trying to catch my breath.

"Thank you," I croaked at Yearlove."

13

PLACES

THE CLOCK TOWER

A prominent setting throughout Avis's first few years at Hailing Hall...

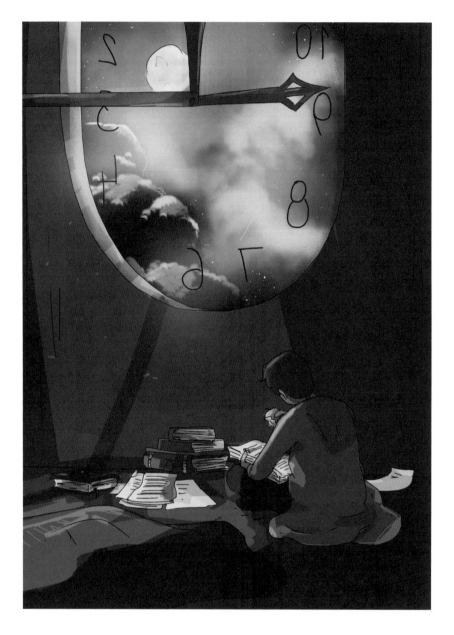

"I returned to my new favourite place, the clock tower. It was set up high in the spire. And no one came up here, ever, they couldn't anyway. I only found it by accident when having a hunt around near the dark turret room. Both clock faces are see-through, so I can see everything that happens from both sides of the courtyard and the gardens. It's weird watching people because I get sad that I can't join them. I found it hidden behind a large tapestry in one of the long corridors near my turret. The first night I sat still listening to the satisfying clicks of the metal clockwork and watching the sun setting over the horizon. Then I couldn't stand going back to the small, dank turret, so I collected all my stuff and moved into the clock tower. At least here I had a view, some light and no Magisteers coming to check up on me every other day unannounced. I mean, it wasn't perfect, the bells rang deafening loud at certain times, there was a flock of pigeons up in the rafters that pooed all the time, and it was incredibly dusty, but it sure felt homely."

THE CLOCK TOWER is one of the highest points in the school and has two glass paned clock faces, so Avis can see out of them. In first year, Avis is accused of setting a demon on his friend and form mate Hunter — for this, he is ostracised and barred from the rest of the school and asked to stay in a tower away from everyone, until they figure out what actually happened. But Avis didn't like the dank tower, so he found the clock tower near by and stayed there instead. It was bigger, brighter and he could see out the glass clock faces.

IN HIS SECOND YEAR, Avis returns there, to do a bad deed — release the Djinn from the incense holder, in return for a wish.

And he is back there again, hiding, when the wish (the jumper) goes bad and people won't leave him alone. He just wanted to be liked, but when the jumper got spiked and frayed, so did the magic. The popularity turned into madness, even Tina was not immune and chased Avis around the clock tower, until Jasper stopped it.

You can just make out the bridge across to the floating island from one of the clock faces.

FLOATING ADVENTURE PLAY AREA

There are many surprises around Hailing Halls grounds that you would be surprised to learn about. But a floating adventure play area? Well yes indeed. It's one of the biggest adventure play area's in the world, and sits on a bed of cloud — don't be fooled though, if you fall off, the magic cloud won't help you. You will fall through the cloud and hurt yourself. You must use magic to think quickly and soften your fall.

LOST PROPERTY ROOM

A mysterious and prominent room located within the dungeons of Hailing Hall. Avis is first taken their a few days into his starting at Hailing Hall, when he needs to collect an ever-changing robes, tie and channeller — which is where he first gets his hands on Malakai's old channeller.

WE SEE the Lost Property Room again when Avis, Robin and Tina do the revealing spell upon Tina's skeleton key and see Ernie Partington pretending to be a Magisteer and breaking his way into the room.

IT'S a room where all the magical artefacts that are found around school, that have no owner, go. The ghosts occasionally tidy the place up, but mainly it's a messy, unorganised mass of hundreds of years of magical stuff. Some, who go there, would see it as a treasure trove.

"THE DEATH CORRIDOR"

Mentioned in Avis's second year, when he and Straker are out looking for the Djinn. It's described as a long corridor, but its actually more of a bridge between the east and west parts of the school. It's a perilous bridge, and known as being treacherous, and is held up, almost exclusively by magic.

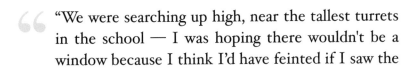

"We were searching up high, near the tallest turrets in the school — I was hoping there wouldn't be a window because I think I'd have feinted if I saw the drop. Straker and I stood before, what everyone in the school had dubbed '*the death corridor*' — it was just any other normal corridor, except for the fact that it was as high up as you could get, very old, and held up exclusively by magic. When looked at from below, the death corridor looked unsafe, suspended in mid-air between two turrets. It was the only way to get across to the other side of the school — this high up anyway."

14

FORMS OF HAILING HALL

THE CONDORS

Each form group has a badge, animal, colours and a specific identity. As you can see with the Condors badge below, the animal is a Condor, the colours (which they use for Riptide) are yellow and black — altogether this gives them their identity within Hailing Hall. It's important for everyone at Hailing Hall to feel like they belong, and so in having forms with their own histories, they always have a home among their form mates.

THE CONDOR FORM has a long history in Hailing Hall, and was one of the original seven forms.

It's customary to get a picture at the end of your first year at Hailing Hall together as a form group — and I think this one summarised them all quite nicely.

(From left to right, top: Avis, Robin, Simon, Dennis, Magisteer Partingon, Ellen, Graham, Joanna. Bottom: Jake, Gret, Dawn, Florence, Jess, Hunter.)

"YOUR FORM IS YOUR FAMILY" is repeated throughout ones time at Hailing Hall and it's true. Your forms mates are chosen very carefully, by a magic decider, who can feel personalities and how they best mix in a form together. It tries to make a form of balanced individuals. You've got to remember some of them will be spending 24 hours a day with each other for years, so it's best they get on. But not all families do.

AVIS'S FIRST IMPRESSION OF HIS FORM MATES...

"We were swiftly given our form name and table. Through sheer luck and good fortune, myself, Robin and Hunter were all in the same form, we were *The Condors*. We sat at this large round table in the middle of the Chamber. Also joining our table, one by one were: Graham, a "Scottish" boy from the Outside. Jess, this red-lipped, pure white-faced girl who looked like she might break if you dropped her. Florence, a girl with loads of freckles. Dennis, a short funny looking lad who spoke so quickly it was hard to understand him. Ellen, this shy girl with large glasses and long poker straight hair. Jake and his twin sister Grettle, I'd never seen identical twins before, especially not a boy and girl one. They were both blond, with green eyes and this kind of naughty, mischievous look. I wasn't sure if I liked it, they sat side by side laughing intermittently as if passing each other telepathic messages. The last four were Simon, a plain-looking boy from

Happendance like me. Joanna, a girl who looked like she belonged more in the woods as her flyaway bushy brown hair would otherwise indicate. Then Dawn, a very large girl who was munching on a box of chocolate raisins."

AVIS'S other form mates play a big role in his first two years at Hailing Hall — obviously Robin plays one of the biggest in saving his life. But in order of the photograph above;

SIMON AND AVIS do not get on, for some reason they have a mutual discord and can't seem to remain civil to one another. It all started when Simon was surprised that Avis got scared by a ghost in the middle of the night (ghosts are very common in wizarding worlds), and with Avis being a Blackthorn and what-not, he proceeds to wind Avis up about this at most available opportunities.

DENNIS STARTED off in first year as being a squeaky, small boy who liked to hang around with girls, but in second year he grows colossally to be one of the biggest in his form.

ELLEN IS A QUIET, bookish girl with large glasses — you could almost say she was the girl version of Robin — and she is very academic.

GRAHAM IS a Scottish boy from the Outside, he and Robin share a carriage home as it's not far from each others houses. He is a brash, loud and outspoken, as boys can be at that age, but a fiercely loyal friend. He also has a tendency towards squandering all his gold on silly bets.

JOANNA IS the bushy haired one on the end, she loves Riptide and captains their team for school matches, her only dream is to one day play professionally. Will she manage it?

JAKE IS A TWIN. At first he struggled being away from his sister Grettle as boys and girls have different rooms, but soon became accustomed to his new friends. He and his sister are from Golandria, and didn't even speak very good English when they arrived, so he and his sister's journey was perhaps one of the most rewarding.

GRET TOO, found a new home with the girls, but finds comfort working alongside her brother — twins, in the magical world, are known to have extra talents. She and her brother love Riptide.

DAWN IS A LARGE GIRL, with an annoying personality, often speaking with her mouth open or blurting out something inappropriate, but at heart, she is a good wizard.

FLORENCE AND JESS always hang around each other, they are the prettiest girls in the form and don't they just know it — they have formed a small clique of girls from other forms who hang around at break times and talk about magic-makeup, boys, and how hot Magisteer Yearlove is.

LASTLY, Hunter; he is fat by his own admission, but he just loves his food, and sleep. He often speaks out at inappropriate times. He is accident prone, and likes getting into trouble. Perhaps that's what got him into the mess in first year — he is also very prideful — when their form was beaten, or rather humiliated by the Eagles at Riptide, he, Avis and Robin decided to get their revenge on the Eagles by dressing up as Malakai and scaring the bejeezus out of them. It almost worked too, until the real Malakai showed up and set a demon on Hunter which ripped his face apart. He recovered though.

THE OTHER FORMS OF HAILING HALL:

HUBRIS

Colours: white and pink.

Notes: The form of Tina Partington and her friends; Tow Taylor Smith, Karma Zhu and Jessie Emms.

EAGLES

Colours: red.

Notes: The form of David Starlight, Avis's nemesis throughout the first year.

SWILLOWS

Colours: white.

Notes: The form of Jasper Gandy, Avis's nemesis throughout the second and third year.

SNARES

Colours: green and white.

Notes: The form of Zara Faraday and Sophie, Avis and Robin's friends throughout the second year.

PHOENIX

Colours: Orange and yellow.

Notes: The form that Ernie joins for his last year at the end of the Avis's first year at Hailing Hall. Tutored by Magisteer Nottingham.

CENTAURS

Colours: Gold

Notes: The form of Marshall Compton-Campbell, Jenson Zhu and Gemma Icke — the best trio in the schools Riptide history.

OTHER FORMS:

- Jaloofias
- Hesserbouts
- Twiddlegawks
- Manticores

- Werewolfs
- Paranders
- Happerbats
- Mermaids
- Lockerdo's
- Flinkydots
- Amfiby
- Colubra

❧ 15 ❧

GHOSTS

Q: Who makes the food at Hailing Hall?
A: The ghosts!

The ghosts at Hailing Hall do all the jobs around the castle that would cost too much gold (or money) to employ people to do. Anyway, ghosts love having things to do, wouldn't you if you had an eternity stuck on Earth?

ONE OF THEIR main duties is the cooking. The kitchens are situated below the Chamber, in the dungeons, which Avis knows because he had to do a detention down there. Through a drape in the Hall there is a slope that goes down into the entrance to the kitchens, which are humungous, like a cathedral, with lots of surfaces for cutting and preparing the food. At one end of the room are huge, fiery ovens.

THE TOLLO TABLE is a ghostly table that sits in one corner of the room — it's very big and the ghosts regard is almost sacredly. When the food is cooked they place it on the Tollo Table, it then shoots upwards through the ceiling and into the Chamber. So, the food does not just 'appear' as some ignorant fellows would state, but rather, is made to appear.

THE GHOSTS also do all the laundry, which is a big but important job — as they don't sleep they take the night as an opportunity to enter the bedrooms, keeping as dim as possible, and collecting all the dirty clothes from the piles they should have been left in, taking them away to be washed and sorted, before being returned by morning clean, dry and folded, as if by magic!

SOME DIFFERENCES IN TASTE...

Newt eye popcorn, is served up at Riptide matches for a small cost. Lets be clear for all the politically correct, they are not real newt eyes. In times past they were, but now they use other things.

ROAST DANDY IS A BIRD, commonly served up on Christmas day. We have Turkey, they have Dandy. A Dandy bird is a long legged magical bird, exclusive to the magical world.

KIWI JUICE IS VERY POPULAR, as it grows like weeds in the vast plains of Lundoria.

MANGO PERRY. It's not alcoholic as the name would suggest, even in wizarding worlds, the drinking age (except for Golandria) is 16. Mango perry has a soothing effect, upon aches and pains or this may just have been clever marketing.

"THE TWITCH"

 "You're not to know," said the ghost before taking

out a small cloth and wiping his ghostly glasses. "A little lesson in food and magic... the two cannot mix. It's dangerous. Food is information, energy, vibration. Its this that sustains a Wizard. You cannot even use magic near or around food for it will then be contaminated. Ingesting magic is serious for a Wizard. It can cause serious health problems. You'll get the *Twitch* for one."

"What's that?" I said.

"The Twitch? A disease that you get when you ingest too much magic. It's very nasty. Mostly, it's prisoners, or the trapped, or the homeless who develop the Twitch. If you are without food, what do you do? You will get it any way you can, and that means using an illusion of food to feel full. There's nothing worse than hunger." I found myself nodding. "We are very careful to make sure we use no magic around our food here. Look..." he pointed to the translucent table with the trays of food set out on it. "The Tollo Table for example is a ghost invention, it uses no Wizard magic at all. It's simply spirit. And yet, there is still stupidity around. I mean look at this..." He handed us a clipping of a newspaper from the wall. "Read that."

MAGIC AND FOOD, CAN WE SAFELY COMBINE?

Jeffery Sanderson, the health minister of Western Happendance has reopened the debate on using magic in food production. For millennia it's been taboo within the Wizarding society, but Sanderson reckons a safe way can be found to aid the slow production. The debate rises after last year was the worst crop yield in a century leading some to question the rising price of food. "If we can experiment and find a way of safely integrating the production of our food with magic that would surely be good for everyone. Cheaper food means more people can afford to eat and eat well. A Wizard cannot last on the measly diet that the minimum gold allowance permits. It's not possible, something must be done."

"The Twitch costs our Healing rooms nearly eight million gold peices a year," says Susan Kennedy of the Council of Healers. "But the homeless and hungry need to eat. It's a tricky dilemma."

"This debate should be off the table," says Golandrian celebrity Jack Hummingbird. "We all know the effects of this awful combination. We need to look at new ways of producing enough food, not ridiculous ways like this. We might as well cast illusions of full banquet tables for all the hungry and be done with it. A tax on the very rich would be a start, they don't need all that gold do they? Surely they can spare a little more? And then we can close this ridiculous debate down once and for all."

OTHER FUNCTIONS OF THE GHOSTS...

But the ghosts don't just do the laundry and cook the food. There are several known ghosts that are stuck in the school. Some are ex-students who died (*think*; Ernie Partington), and others are hiding in the schools many dis-used classrooms. They do also like to get involved in the celebrations, and no such occasions sums this up than the end of year celebration and the seventh years leaving ceremony...

> "Ghosts floated into the Chamber in one mass of white and blue glowing light as suits of armour around the side of the Chamber began blowing on

wind instruments that appeared out of nowhere. We all applauded as loud as we could, as the seventh years, through lots of tears and hugging, slowly began to make their way out of Hailing Hall, as, surprisingly, the ghosts began singing!

We thank you for you time with us,
We hope you've learned your fill,
It's your time now to enter the world,
And make it a better place, still.
Take all that you've learned here and turn it into good,
Make people's lives and all their strives properly
*   understood.*
Go forth now all equal,
We give you our thanks,
Now you are a part of the schools sequel,
Go join your new ranks.
For all that you taught this place,
We thank you,
Forever learn and live with grace,
We hope you've learned your fill,
It's your time now to enter your the world
And make it a better place still..."

16

HEALERS ROOM

THE HEALERS ROOM is the go to place for healing oneself after an accident. It's occupied by the live-in Healer, a beautiful woman with long blonde hair — she's almost otherworldly in her beauty. She looks after anyone who has hurt themselves, which with magic, is quite often. Using Infusions, Charms and spells to heal and repair, everyone leaves feeling better.

There is one major, odd addition to the Healers room that won't find anywhere else; the Sun. There is a Sun that hangs in the middle of the room, it's a dull sun about 12 feet wide that shines a dull green colour. Thus, it's called the Jade Sun. Jade is the shade of green that it emits. It's rays of sun are healing, providing much needed nutrients and light that the energy body of the wizard craves.

AVIS RUNNING INTO THE HEALER'S ROOM FOR THE FIRST TIME, AFTER HEARING ABOUT TINA:

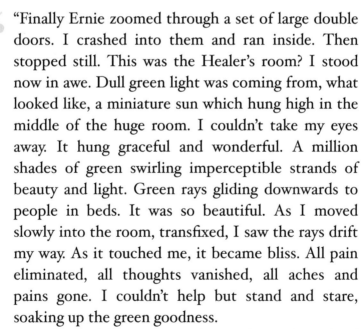

"Finally Ernie zoomed through a set of large double doors. I crashed into them and ran inside. Then stopped still. This was the Healer's room? I stood now in awe. Dull green light was coming from, what looked like, a miniature sun which hung high in the middle of the huge room. I couldn't take my eyes away. It hung graceful and wonderful. A million shades of green swirling imperceptible strands of beauty and light. Green rays gliding downwards to people in beds. It was so beautiful. As I moved slowly into the room, transfixed, I saw the rays drift my way. As it touched me, it became bliss. All pain eliminated, all thoughts vanished, all aches and pains gone. I couldn't help but stand and stare, soaking up the green goodness.

A beautiful woman in a long, white robe walked elegantly towards me. Her blonde hair hung down to her ankles, her face radiant, with eyes the same green as the sun. And then she spoke with an angelic, soothing voice. "You are here to see Tina Partington?"

"Yes... wait, Partington?" something else smacked me in the face. Tina's and Ernie's Dad was... my form tutor... Magisteer Partington?!

Ernie was bobbing up and down near a bed in the corner of the room. "This way," said the Healer.

Tina lay unconscious. Green rays coarsing in and out of each breath. She looked bad. Open wounds lit her face scarlet red and her hair was matted with dried blood. The soft white clothes she had been put running red. The Healer dabbed at the wounds with a white cloth, soaked in a bowl of water and soft smelling potions. As the green light and the water touched her face, the wounds knitted back together. It was strange to watch. Her beautiful face returning in some part back to the one I knew. Tears welled up in my eyes now at the sight of her. Her words reverberating around my mind from the last time she spoke to me. Ernie bobbed by her bedside, sobbing into her pillow.

"All my fault," he mumbled."

17

MAGICAL CREATURES

The magical world is a home to all the magical creatures that exist in your mythical knowledge. Things like fairies, leprechauns, gnomes and elves, all exist within the magical world. It is said that when the magical lands were created, these creatures (so called as they are humanoid in nature) signed up to join the wizards, who understand the elementals, and lay claim to their owns lands. They no longer wanted to share the earth with humans who attacked them and treated them badly. Only wizards, who were also persecuted by religious nutted humans, understood the elementals.

LEPRECHAUNS

They are 3 feet tall, dress always in green which is a colour that corresponds to the lands that they thrive upon and reminds them of their fatherlands of Ireland. They left Ireland after being run out by humans and found a new home in the Seven Magical Kingdoms. The myths in legend and law are correct, they are obsessed with gold and run an almost seamless operation to hunt, mine and procure gold. They never steal, they only lay claim to gold left behind, with no owner, or gold that lays in mines.

GNOMES ARE SIMPLE CREATURES, who live in burrows, usually if they are lazy, old rabbits burrows. They are only 1 feet tall and do not mix with leprechauns very well at all. They are mischievous and set out to cause as much trouble as they can.

ELVES ARE an offshoot of fairies and are in the same family. They are very rare, some people having never seen them would say they do not exist. But they do. They are clever, shy and complicated creatures. They look human in looks with bright white skin like snow. You can spot an Elf, by their ears, which are slightly pointed at the top.

THIS IS *an except from the Herrald, in which Avis reads:*

> The front page of the Herrald was pretty boring, something about Sorcerers refusing to pay tax, and the leprechauns scrounging off the Magical Council. I never really read newspapers before, but I felt quite civilised as I sat there nibbling a croissant, sipping my tea and thumbing through the Herrald. There was some good stuff too, this is what I learnt:
> * The pig people who are in charge of all the gold want to go on strike because they are not allowed massive gold bonus's.
> * Mr. Wolfe, the conductor on my train is up in court, responsible for biting a piggy banker (the consensus seemed to be that he was more of a hero than a villain, even though the judge was a piggy.)
> * Malakai and his supporters had stormed a local council in Gilliggan and taken it over, (so that's what my parents had been up to).
> Robin was very interested about anything Magical and asked me constant questions whenever they popped into his head. He was fascinated with that fact that I was born into the Magical world. Over breakfast he seemed to think of more questions, perhaps the newspaper had sparked a few more ideas.
> "So do you have different races or species in your Magical Kingdoms?"
> "Yes," I said sagely, folding the newspaper.

"There's the pig people, leprechauns, fauns, Imps, Gnomes, erm... loads really."

"Cor, in my world, we were always taught that those things were made up, myths and fairytales."

"Yeah, course you were," I laughed. "Who do you think wants you to think there a myth?" He looked at me blankly. "We do of course, there's more of you than there are of us."

THE PIGGIES ARE PIG-PEOPLE. Pig's that have become

humanoid. They play their role within the magical kingdoms, although they are not regarded highly by wizards, who tolerate them at best. They are selfish, greedy and cowardly. You will find the piggies working with gold, banking, in fact anything which involves money.

THEIR EXISTENCE, like most humanoid creatures came about most likely due to magical experimentation on the part of wizards, by accident, or by continually surrounded with magic, which transformed them into humanoid creatures.

Mr Wolfe, is a humanoid wolf. His family has been written about in folklore of humans, let alone wizards. Mr Wolfe comes from a long line of walking, talking wolves, called the Wolfice race. They and the piggies do not get on whatsoever, owing to the fact the Mr Wolfe keeps trying to eat them.

18

MAGICAL ANIMALS

Magical animals are different to *creatures*. Magical animals exist solely in the magical lands and will not venture out into human lands, which they see and fear as dangerous.

WASPERATS

Are half a foot in size — and a cross between a wasp and a rat. It can fly, sting, bite and pest. They have red eyes and are very greedy. They buzz about with short stubby wings, which can sometimes barely keep them up if they've eaten a large meal.

SPRATS

Magical wing-less rats, these too have red eyes but do walk on two legs and are slightly cleverer than their Outsider counterparts, the rats, and also have a moderate amount of magical talent, which they use mainly to pinch food.

KREDE HOPPERS

They look and sound like frogs and for all intents and purposes, they are. Except, they have a special talent of being able to walk on water. Or rather; hop across water. Krede, in wizarding old language, meant water.

TALKING TURTLES

Just like our turtles, except these ones can talk — apart from droning on about history and lettuce they are not that useful or interesting.

WOLFRAPTORS

Cross your fingers you'll never see one. They are scary creatures. Stealthy like a ninja, cunning like a fox and vicious like a tiger, they have fur wings that can stretch twenty feet, razor sharp teeth and a howl that will send shivers down a ghosts spine.

FLORAX

A two foot tall devilishly naughty creature that likes to collect teeth, fallen out or not. It can morph into light, like an angel.

HAPPERBATS

Wizard thieves used them to sneak into houses and steal the shiniest most valuable items. They like shiny things and antiques
    They are like bats, but they can't fly far. They can see in the dark.

PARANDERS

Large majestic creatures with white, silvery skin. They live in shallow pools of water. Have a horn on the end of it's nose and only eats fish and algae. It can turn itself invisible in a second.

HUBRIS

Is a large, thick skinned, quite blind animal — akin to a Rhino,
but with the best sense of smell on the planet. They can smell

your entire life and will know everything about you. A quite revered and intelligent animal. They get scared by people. But are very gentle and spiritual if you can get one to build trust in you.

UNFORTUNATELY, they are killed and their skin is used in lots of wizarding wares. The hubris leather is quite magical, it can repel spells and charms, it can hide things inside it and sells for quite a pretty penny. However, there is a movement to stop them being killed.

FARADAY

Used by the postal service to deliver items to peoples houses.
They have the ability to zap across great distances. They
mostly fly, but can jump a few miles at a time by *zapping* in a
puff of fire and appearing in the air a few miles away. When

ordering something, it will appear in your house, drop off the parcel and then you must place gold into it's mouth — it will not leave until you have done so, in fact if you don't pay it will attack.

AN OFFSHOOT OF A DRAGON, it's said, it can grow to the size of a small carriage (or car) and be quite dangerous.

Avis came into contact with one when ordering from the wizarding catalogue...

    "Running as fast as I could, I barged back into my room. Why did this have to happen to me? For a moment, everything was going brilliantly — and then, like all the other friends I had made before him, Sedrick too, had run away.

I steadied myself and tried to think of a way out of this — the only thing I could do was find a way to follow Sedrick. A ripple of worry tickled my stomach, I had absolutely no idea where he had gone... I mean, it could be anywhere!

SMASH! My piggy bank oinked one last time, as shards of porcelain scattered the floor. Shame, I liked that piggy bank. I had to pull it out of a hole in the floor, covered by a stone — my secret hiding place where I stashed everything I didn't want my evil siblings to get a hold of. Otherwise, these ten gold coins wouldn't last a second.

Ten gold coins? What could that buy me?

I jumped across and grabbed a copy of the Sogra Catalouge— it's like this big book that sells all sorts of magical items. I needed something that could help me find Sedrick... *flick, flick, flick* through the pages I went in quiet desperation.

The floor was kicking up dust as I paced, awaiting the delivery of my order — it shouldn't be much longer. An hour tops. That was the good thing about ordering from Sogra, you didn't have to wait long for them to deliver.

There was a sudden flash of green and blue light in the middle of the room. I stepped back as a large, brown parcel appeared.

Bwarrrrk!

On top of the parcel was the faraday. It was a greeny-blue kind of animal about the size of a cat, but kind of dinosaur looking with small wings, a triangular head and vicious teeth. They always sent faradays with parcels now, to make sure people paid. It snapped its mouth at me as I approached fast and started ripping the brown paper off.

"AHA!" I cried, before pulling out a large, shining crystal ball — *'The Specto 120'* — the best in it's cheaper price range — don't judge me, it's all I could afford. I placed the crystal ball on my bed before ripping the paper off the rest of the stuff, including:

Some vanishing salt.

A book called *The Beginners Guide to Forms of Travel*, which was about salt rings and travelling between different worlds.

And finally some *Sally Juniper's Wiggly Worm Sweets* — I needed the energy. It was probably going to be a long night!

I pulled one out, which squirmed in my fingers before placing the writhing thing in my mouth. *Mmmm...* anyway, to work!

Bwarrrk! Went the faraday again, snapping its long beak at me.

"What do you want?" I said a little impatiently. Big mistake, it went for me!

Bwarrrk! Bwarrrk! Bwarrrk!

"Ahh!" I cried, jumping back on my bed as the faraday lunged at me with vicious long teeth. "Okay, okay!" I called — putting my hand in my pocket and pulling out the ten gold coins, before reluctantly placing them in its mouth.

Bwarrrk. It went, satisfied. Before going back to the middle of the room and vanishing in a blast of blue and green.

Pesky thing."

BIGLOBEAR

A Biglobear is a small, dumb looking bear that lives in the trees of Happendance. They sleep and eat, and that's about it. However, as with most magical animals, there is a bite in the tail. They can and will attack — if one eats strawberries, or eats past midnight on a full moon, it will grow to the size of a house, be extremely angry and kill anything in sight. It will eat an entire village, and has been known to eat Dragons. When it changes back to itself it will poo out a tiny, perfectly round nugget that will be extraordinarily heavy. And will sometimes sink so far down into the earth as to create a huge hole.

CENTAURS

You could argue that Centaurs are actually creatures, as they are mainly, humanoid. However, as they have four legs they are considered animals — which they are not happy about and want the same rights as wizards. They are a warrior race and keep to themselves in the forests of the Seven Magical Kingdoms.

Extremely proficient in archery, they can shoot a moving target from miles away. There bow-craft skills are the best in the world, they can create a bow, woven with their magic, that can shoot a self-aiming arrow that will always hit the target, they in high demand but will not sell to wizards, no matter what the price.

They also have a great knowledge of astrology, astromagic, geometry and leylines.

19

MAGICAL ITEMS OF THE MAGICAL WORLD

THE SEVEN LEAGUE SHOES

Avis has a pair of Seven League Shoes. They are ancient, and he thought mythical, pair of shoes that allow one to travel extremely quickly across lands. For every step you take, the shoes will carry you ten. It gives the appearance that you are an extra fast runner, but only you, the wearer, can see the golden light beneath your feet as you sprint away at the speed of light.

AVIS FIRST SAW them in the underground passageway that Malakai used in the school in his first year. But then, as a reward for what he did, the Lily gifted them to Avis, knowing that he would find them useful. And he does, they play a great role in him escaping from numerous situations.

Avis and Magisteer Straker sprinting out of the Death Corridor as it collapses.

THE STORY *of the Seven League Shoes:*

An hour later I let out another soft *"Harrah!"*

"What is it?" said Robin dropping his book. "Found something?"

"Oh, of course!" I said, slapping the side of my head. The book I was reading was called *Magical Myths, Hidden and Real in Fairytales: #3 — Magical Artefacts.* "This is so weird. I opened this book and it just fell open at this page..." I turned the big, crusty book towards him pointing at the title. "Listen to this...

> *Alice Norton, the inventor of the only original pair of Seven League Boots, sold her blueprint to the mad inventor Septimus Libramus, a fair man who presided justice over Southern Farkingham in the mid-1830's. Seeing the potential in boots that could help you travel many miles in merely a few steps, Septimus set about making them for the mass market, his dream being that all should be able to travel wherever they must at will.*
>
> *But, after producing and selling just seven pairs, a Wizard who had taken offence at one of Septimus' justice rulings, burnt his house down, with him in it. Alice Norton's original blueprint was destroyed. Before anyone could track down Alice Norton, who had taken a spell of anonymity, she died (at the age of 92), taking her magic boot blueprint with her to the grave.*
>
> *Thus comes the fairytale 'Septimus's Special Shoes':*

Septimus walked on creaking bones barely far enough
    that day,
'If only I could have a pair of shoes that could walk for
    me', he'd say
So, off he set, on a journey to find that magic,
Over many miles he trod, with each step his dream
    enlarged,
Neglecting his duties as justice-giver,
And promoting his apprentice who was barely able.
But one day he found what he'd always hoped,
In a little village with cottages and such,
He stayed at the inn, where he ate and drank,
Listening to the conversation of the village folk,
Who laughed about the mad old woman who ran
    everywhere,
'How can she run so fast at such age?' they'd say.
Septimus listened intently this way —
Gathering an idea of the old woman from number 13.
Of the magic he was convinced, she was no fraud.
She let him try out the boots on himself, of which he was
    amazed,
He offered her all the gold he had for the plans she
    had made,
She accepted barely one coin, and gave him the plans.
And a borrow of the boots, saying
he should bring them back when he had studied
    enough,
She pointed to the heels and said: "Tap-tap to go. Tap-tap
    to stop,
Wear them now, and be home in a pop..."

 I stopped reading. I'd never heard this fairytale, but it sure added up in my brain as memories were zipping around my mind piecing together like a puzzle.

"So?" said Robin shrugging. "It's just a story?"

"Didn't you spot it? At the end?" I said incredulous. "Listen, the last time I zoomed off, was when Hunter clipped my heels. The time before that I tripped up. Like it says here, *Tap-tap to go. Tap-tap to stop.*"

"*Ahhh*, I get it. The famous *double tap,*" said Robin leaning back wistfully. "Of course!"

20

TAITS WALKING BOOKCASE

Taits Walking Bookcase is an item sold in the back pages of the Herrald. It's a piece of wood that fits into your breast pocket, but then when you want to use it, you simply pull it out (making sure you have enough space), and it grows into a full size bookcase, which can walk around after you. It expands to fit the number of books you have.

AVIS WANTS to buy this for Robin at the end of the first year, but cannot afford it. So he gifts him something he finds instead...

THE 'EFFY-RAY SPECTACLES'.

Effervescent-ray spectacles come under a variety of different names. First mentioned at the end of Avis's first year, when he finds them in the passageway that Malakai was using in the school. They, most probably, used to belong to him too. So Avis gifted them to Robin, who wears glasses anyway. But these are extra special, they allow one to see magic in the air around them. Spells become illuminated — long strands of colour stretching through the corridors. The brighter the colour, the more recent the spell was done, the dimmer the colour means the further back in time.

ROBIN IS CONVINCED by Avis to wear them for Riptide. Which is a mistake. Robin can see the Ornaments around the Habitat which grants them several victories. But this is found out at the end of the year and they are banned from playing Riptide for the third year.

"Just before dinner that night, in the Condor dorm, I told Robin to wait behind.

"What? What is it?" Robin said, looking worried.

I laughed. "Nothing to worry about mate."

"Oh right," he said. "Good, no more drama please."

"I erm, just wanted to give you this," I pulled out the little wrapped parcel from under my bed and gave it to him.

"For me? Why?"

"Why? *Why?* For saving my life? For bringing back two dead people in record time!" I said as he smiled. He took the parcel and unwrapped it, pulling out a pair of old, wire framed spectacles.

"Now, they don't look like much," I said. "But these are a pair of..."

"I know what they are," he gasped. "Wow, thank you mate, but... where did you get them?"

"Secret. I just never got to properly thank you, cos' you know you were the *real saviour* that night. If it hadn't been for you... well."

He swapped his glasses for the spectacles. "Woah!" he called, jumping backwards. "Weird! I couldn't wear these all the time!"

"I know right, weird aren't they!" I'd tried them on in the passageway. When you put them on, they revealed every bit of Magic that had been done in the vicinity. The most recent Magic shows up bright and colourful, whereas historical Magic shows up faded and grey. It makes your eyes hurt seeing all the bright colours of recent Magic, but immensely useful and cool if you know what your looking at.

21

SKELETON KEY

In Avis's first year at Hailing Hall, in the middle of the night, he finds Tina creeping around the school — this is when Avis and Robin find out about her quest, to get revenge upon the evil Malakai. Around her neck is a key made of white bone... a magical skeleton key which can unlock any door. They are much fabled throughout history and are even rare in the wizarding world. Where she got it is a mystery too, for they could be sold for a lot of gold.

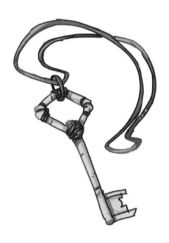

HIDDEN INK

This is one of the main prizes that Hailing Hall gives out for good work. Amongst other useful things like pots of normal ink, pens and quills, parchment books, that kind of thing.

HOWEVER, Hidden Ink is a special form of ink. You write as you normally would, the words appear in black on the page — however, a second or two later, the words vanish. This is especially useful for passing secret messages to people and were used extensively to pass messages to one another in war times. There are a variety of different ways you can reveal the words — the first is to pour a whole bottle in a shallow tray, then dip the sheet of parchment into it, slowly the words reveal themselves. You can put more magic on it too, so only one person can read the hidden words.

22

CHANNELLERS

They are a powerful bit of magic. Channellers are an item of jewellery, most commonly; amulets, pendants, rings and necklaces, that allow you to channel your magic more safely than without. Before the invention of channellers and the requirement by magical law to only do magic through them, wizards did not use them and risk blowing their spark (which is to kill your magic and no longer be able to do it) but also to blow up everyone around them.

LATER ON, they began to realise that wood was an especially good conduit for magic, and certain kinds of wood, like willow. But these slowly fell out of fashion a hundred years ago. They realised that certain metals had the same, if not far greater abilities to channel and hold magic, allowing for greater speed, accuracy and guile. So metal wands became all the rage. Some even went to far as to include quartz crystals in their metal wands, which allowed for enhancements to their magic. But then a man called Gilbert Gun, went against the fashion of the time and insisted on having his wand attached to him via a magic chain — he was a notorious dueller, and this allowed him the advantage of not losing it, his wand being stolen nor it being expelled from his grip by a spell.

NOWADAYS, channellers are filled with the crushed crystals of one or several different quartz stones. They say that every channeller is different, and that is true. A quartz stone has very different effects upon a wizard, for instance an obsidian quartz will help a Sagittarius wizard whose numerological number is 4.

EACH WIZARD, depending on their birth date, astrological sign, numerological value and personality will have a metal that they are sympathetic with (this means, the metal likes them) and the same with different quartz stones which match and help the personality of the wizard. So, when they go looking for a channeller, they will often find their 'one' (as it's said there is only 'one' out their for each person) through a series of coincidences. They will know it's theirs by right as the channeller will do something in the shop like light up or cast a shot of smoke, or something strange.

23

CARRIAGES

Magical carriages look just like carriages from the Outside, which were used predominantly throughout history. Wizards use very victorian looking carriages and their styles vary according to which kingdom you are from. Golandrian's prefer gothic looking carriages with mullioned gas lamps and black lace. Happendancian's don't particularly care and Slackerdown's are always white.

> "A carriage is a wheeled vehicle for people, usually horse-drawn. The carriage is especially designed for private passenger use and for comfort or elegance, though some are also used to transport goods. It may be light, smart and fast or heavy, large and comfortable. Carriages normally have suspension using leaf springs, elliptical springs (in the 19th century) or leather strapping."

HORSE DRAWN ONES are most common. These use partially flying carriages, but are effectively blind and cannot fly un-aided, so they do so with the addition of flying horses. These horses are magical and come from Lundoria, they are complete diva's and only eat wild-grass from Lundoria.

IF YOU ARE RICH, like the Blackthorns are, you can afford a self-flying carriage.

"Then, my carriage shot into the air so fast I thought I might have left my stomach on the school grounds. I leant out the window and waved to my friends. My best friends. Tall, clever, be speckled Robin. The taller, handsome, charismatic Ernie. And of course, the teary, mad, beautiful Tina.

Maybe someone up there does like me, before I started school, I wished more than anything to make a friend. And, well, I'd made three of the best friends I could have ever wished for. In a few seconds they turned into mere specs. We hit the rainbow and multi coloured glitter filled the carriage. The sky was full of carriages like a flock of black birds dancing above a fountain of exploding Magical fireworks."

24

THE BOOK OF NAMES

The following passage is from Avis's first year, in which he, Robin and Hunter are searching through the library after hours and in which they make several key findings that will lead to them bringing down Malakai...

"After a whole weekend in the Library, I came across a couple of things that I found immensely intriguing. The first was a simple but quite brilliant Spell. I nearly yelped with surprise when I found it hidden in a book all about water creatures...

"... to approach these creatures who sense humans by their thought frequencies given off by the brain, a Spell is required which hides this: Avertere, forces whatever looks at you to not register your form. But more, it hides your thought frequencies, which the brain rather haphazardly gives off at all times. The Spell is not full proof, one can be spotted out of the creature's peripheral, this may alert them, but when looked at directly you will not be spotted, thus they think they are seeing things. Immensely useful in approaching marine wildlife, some Wizards have experienced it working well on other Wizards..."

This was a revelation. It meant that now I could walk around, especially to the Library, without being disturbed. But also, I had read that Wizards, mostly the highly trained ones, could sense what you were thinking, and your next move, by reading the thought frequencies that your brain leaks out. What I never knew was, thoughts are emitted as vibrational waves, just like a Spell, or a radio wave, which can be interpreted just like a radio antenna interprets a radio wave and turns it into sound! I had no doubt that Malakai could read thoughts, even people like Partington had a good grasp of it, and the Lily was a master, I was sure. This Spell, would be very useful - especially if I combined it with something else.

This book had several illuminating passages:

True names, discovered in 1243, are commonly misunderstood today. Initially, it was thought, if one found out the true name of a Wizard then you had an all encompassing power over them. In actual fact, this is largely mythical. Knowing one's true name does not give one infinite power. In fact, if you know and say a true name of an enemy, and they know not yours, then whatever Spell you direct at them will trump theirs. You have a huge level of control over them, some say you take over as the master of their destiny, but this is an exaggeration. Merely, where the power lies, is in the sharing of the true name - for if one shared a Wizards name out, the power of the Wizard will wane both physically and actually - great power had lay in knowing a Wizards true name and threatening to share it, this in itself can guarantee their compliance in all you require.

The high Wizard Tyreko, who came to high power in 1655 was sent mad by a past misdeed and killed many Witches. Santi Venart, a training Witch who once knew Tyreko seduced him using love Magic and found out his true name. She shared the name "Egbert Richardsward" far and wide. Overnight, Tyreko reduced in size, shrinking to four feet. He aged fifty years and resembled a swamp creature. He died shortly after, being set upon by roaming vagabonds.

Over the years, many myths and legends have not aided the truth when it comes to true names - some still believe that one who knows ones true name, has the power to send another to a place worse than Hell - a kind of purgatory, or collection centre, that one can store all those whom one knows the true names of. While this might be possible to someone of prestigious talent, it's not likely, or a given whatsoever. True names were brought forth by Magical Nature, to ensure that no one got too powerful... if they did, like Tyreko, there was a means to control them back to safety. This may seem contradictory explanation, True Names are a complicated Magic, and are not to be messed with. Thus the phrase "He needs to be Tyreko-ed" comes.

My head was spinning after reading. I scanned the rest of the book but nothing was as concise as that, but it did go into information about how true names are found...

How Santi Vernart found Tyreko's true name is not known, some say she made him confess to his new love, which would be plausible owing to her extensive practice in love Magic, others think she had help from the infamous Council of Indigo - who have helped end many sent wayward by the effects of black Magic - but some think there is a book, hidden by ancient Magic, that records all true names. It's been referred to under several different names; Gillet's Book of Truth, Hallert and Jivaldo's Newly Born Names, Wizard Namero and simply; The Book of Names, plus many others. Although only myth, many profess that this book is real, many more have seen it - a book by Selibrius Xanderious details that the book travels between twelve unknown locations, every twelve years at the end of a quarter. Many

agree with Selibrius, others state that such an item as
a Book of True names is dangerous, especially in the
wrong hands and should be destroyed."

THE BOOK OF NAMES

Is a most complicated and otherworldly magical item. In the
first year Avis discovers that Malakai is coming into the school
and they set out to find out why. It turns out that he is using the
Book of Names, but due to the book only being available in 12
different certain locations, Malakai must make the journey to it,
not the other way around. The Book, used by Malakai brings
him great power, which Avis helps to stop.

It is a book full of all the names of every wizard born, but
not just their *given name (human name),* which would be Avis
Blackthorn, but also their *True Name*, the name given to them
by magic.

If you learn of a wizards true name, you control that wizard.
If you have access to the Book of Names, you control every
wizard.

But, seventh sons are an exception, they are not in the Book
of Names. This is why Malakai set out to kill all seventh sons.

Avis finds the Book of Names in Malakai's hidden room.

25

THE END OF AVIS BLACKTHORN

A vis gets more than he bargained for when he thinks he is being clever. He thinks that by doing a revealing spell on Tina's channeller that he can see where she last was. In part he was correct, he does see where she went, but he gets a whole lot more...

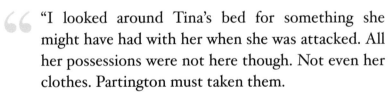

"I looked around Tina's bed for something she might have had with her when she was attacked. All her possessions were not here though. Not even her clothes. Partington must taken them.

But wait... she was wearing a ring, I think it was her channeller. I'd never noticed it much before, but I am sure Partington had one that looked the same. It was silver and slim, with black indentations all the way around. I couldn't make out what but it looked like names.

When the Healer left the room I took Tina's hand. I felt guilty and my heart began racing. I slid the ring off her finger and lay it on the bed next to her. Glancing around, I knew I didn't have long, for the Healer would be back any minute. I raised my shaking hand over the ring and said the Spell.

My head flew back in the chair. But this wasn't right. The vision was surrounded by choking, black smoke. A laughing voice echoed in my head and I saw Tina fall to the floor, Malakai's skeletal frame standing over her. Then his blue glowing eyes looked at me. Awful choking black smoke filled my lungs and I woke. I lifted my head and choked my guts up! Oozing black gunge came out of my mouth and nose. It was like nothing I had ever tasted. I felt sick and ill. Thick green light began to encircle me as I coughed and coughed.

After an hour, I was better. The Healer returned to the commotion and called me an idiot as she put the ring on the side table. She gave me a bowl of stuff to breath in, covering my head with a towel.

"Idiot, idiot..." she kept muttering. "What were you thinking? She's been cursed, all her possessions are cursed. What did you think would happen? Do you think people wiser than you hadn't thought about performing a revealing Spell on her possessions?"

I looked up from under the towel, feeling small... Black goo, not as much as before, was slowly making it's way out of my lungs.

"I'm sorry," I said for the thousandth time. "What?" I whispered. His eyes were fixed on a place just over the rim of the stadium, in the distance. "What Robin?"

He pointed. "It's him."

I followed his gaze. My heart beating fast, as chatter and noise around me faded. Adrenaline began pumping through my body. It was Malakai. Gliding along the surface of the grounds...

THE SHOWDOWN WITH MALAKAI

At the end of Avis's first year, he comes to a showdown with Malakai and he is killed by Malakai. Avis is a Blackthorn, so Malakai gave him a wide berth, but when Avis tries to get in the way of Malakai and the Book of Names he takes action.

AVIS IS KILLED (BY MAGIC), and leaves his body. A hole in the wall opens out and a golden escalator becomes visible, which goes into the starry night sky. Avis takes the escalator and feels happy. But then halfway up he sees Tina's face in the stars and remembers why he tried to thwart Malakai, and then becomes a ghost as he now feels guilt (a heavy human emotion) and thus has unfinished business.

BUT MALAKAI FORGOT ONE THING: if Avis is a ghost, then he is not held back by human spells. He is now free to say Malakai's true name.

"No! Please!" I cried. In an explosive burst of twinkling light, the stars shot towards me. I screamed as light erupted through the room. The pain was unbearable. Every pore in my body on fire. I felt myself writhing on the ground, the room was spinning violently and I could think of was the pain!

And then quiet.

Deadly, heavenly quiet.

I felt my last breath leave me.

I sat up.

Malakai was looking over the book, hunched back rising up and down.

A crack split the wall to the right. White fluorescent light, smattered with transparent mini rainbows, began to fill the room. Malakai hadn't noticed and now I knew why. I was *dead*.

I looked around. I was hovering just above the floor. Below me was my body, lying in a sorry sprawling heap in the dirt. The strange thing was, I wasn't shocked. All my pain was gone, in fact, every pain I had ever had was gone. It was as if I didn't even realise some of the aches and pains I was carrying around with me. All I felt now was a gentle, relaxed, peaceful bliss. My thoughts felt the same.

The crack in the wall widened with a splitting sound, spilling more starry light into the room. A strange noise suddenly came across me as this time, golden light reflected off the walls. A huge golden escalator appeared through the crack. Without thinking, I drifted towards it and stepped on. It moved upwards slowly, through the crack and up into the clouds. The hole in the wall sealed and that sorry room disappeared. All around me was the most wonderful, lustrous twilight with a humungous starry sky with soft clouds moving daintily. The midnight blue spread into violet and indigo the higher we climbed, the texture like that of running paint on parchment.

I turned to look back, but the crack in the wall was but a dot. In the clouds above, a girls sleeping face suddenly appeared. It was Tina. Then I remembered... I was meant to save her... the thought felt foreign. Attached to human emotions I no longer had. Overriding guilt started somewhere where my stomach had been, then spread to my heart area. I felt guilty for leaving her, for she would never know the beauty of death.

The escalator began to jolt and stutter then slow. My thoughts began returning, my form changing. The silky translucent entity I currently was, began curdling. Turning gloopy and wet... I was becoming a ghost. Now I remembered why. The closer the escalator moved back to earth, the quicker my old thoughts returned, hardening in my mind in the same speed that my form took to turn into a ghost.

The book I had read about ghosts said that you become a ghost if you have a strong emotional anchor on Earth. Tina was my emotional anchor and... I had planned that, yes I did, I remembered now. The plan returned in full form into my ghostly mind. I felt kind of flimsy, half in this world, half in another.

The crack in the wall reopened wide beneath me. I stepped off and back into that room as the crack sealed with a snap. Malakai, who was pouring salt in a circle around the Book of Names, now looked round. My ghostly form emitted a blue glow in this dim cave. Then, he laughed a loud piercing cackle. It struck something inside me, hurting me as the blue glow dimmed a little. I concentrated, fighting the urge to float away through the walls and hide.

⚜ 26 ⚜

MAGIC

M agic wouldn't be magic without spells. And to be a great wizard you must have an encyclopaedic knowledge of them.

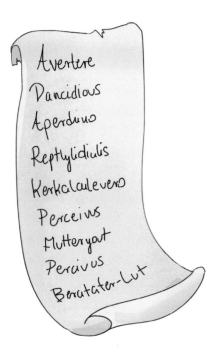

A spells page

THE FOLLOWING SPELLS that are used throughout Avis's time at school are written in the following format:

Spell name
Short description
"Example of the spell being used in the books..."

AVERTERE

To hide oneself

Use this spell to make anyone who tries to look at you, have their gaze mysteriously averted.

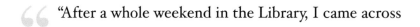 "After a whole weekend in the Library, I came across

a couple of things that I found immensely intriguing. The first was a simple but quite brilliant Spell. I nearly yelped with surprise when I found it hidden in a book all about water creatures...

"... *to approach these creatures who sense humans by their thought frequencies given off by the brain, a Spell is required which hides this:* Avertere, *forces whatever looks at you to not register your form. But more, it hides your thought frequencies, which the brain rather haphazardly gives off at all times. The Spell is not full proof, one can be spotted out of the creature's peripheral, this may alert them, but when looked at directly you will not be spotted, thus they think they are seeing things. Immensely useful in approaching marine wildlife, some Wizards have experienced it working well on other Wizards...*""

DANCIDIOUS

To block another's spell

Dancidious appears, most times, as a black paw that will appear on command and swipe the attackers spell out of the air before it can reach you and have an effect.

AVIS AND ROBIN find this spell by accident when they go searching the Library at night, finding it in an old spell book — this spell comes in great use when Avis uses it to block his brother's spell.

APERCHINO

Offensive wind/fire spell (red)

This is an offensive spell, used to attack another individual, most commonly in a duel. It takes the form of a red bolt of fire, encased by a swirling fast moving spiral of wind.

THESE ARE NOT MEANT to be used on another wizard, but they are common knowledge, like swear words, but are used sparingly.

"Then I felt something wet go right down my front. "*Whoops...*" said a voice. Jasper! I looked down. He'd poured an entire glass of blood orange juice down my front. "That's what happens to those who aren't invited," he spat. I quickly looked around, no one saw, everyone was dancing. "Nice shirt," he smiled.

"How dare you do that to me!" I cried, fury boiling over. Without thinking, I pushed him as hard as I could. He sprawled across the floor falling backwards into some fourth years who dropped their drinks everywhere.

"*WOAH!*" they cried as Jasper jumped up and lunged at me, pushing me to the floor.

I clenched my fist and quickly said: "*Pasanthedine!*" Jasper shot into the air away from me, as I jumped up quickly. Then he smiled, raising his hands, a black shot of smoke punched me hard in the gut.

"Ahh!" I toppled forwards into dancing feet, hugging my stomach. Anger and frustration boiled up inside me. I stood quickly, raising my right hand at his throat and yelled: "*Aperchino!*" red wind burst out of my arm like fire. A satisfied glow lit up inside me, as my skin tingled. I felt myself fall back into the ground with the force as the red wind zapped towards his face. A silvery shield spell erupted in front of him. The red wind bounced off. There was a sudden and colossal *BANG!* As it hit the huge mirror above the fireplace, shattering it into a million pieces."

REPTLYLIDIULIS

Illusion spell

Creates an illusion of a giant, aggressive snake.

Avis finds this spell in his first year, when he Robin and Hunter are searching for ways to scare David Starlight and the Eagles form group.

I looked down at my nails, inspecting them thoroughly. "Oh..." I said gently. "Hello, boys."

It was then that David Starlights voice echoed along the corridor.

"Oi Jason! ... Jason? Steve? What are you guys looking at?" he called in his bullish manor.

As he came round in his spotted pajamas, he circled his frozen friends, then caught their gaze and followed it. He saw me, grinned then as quick as lightning, his whole mouth dropped. Wiped from his face in one swipe. His eyes rolling upwards at the fake Malakai.

I stepped forward and spoke slowly. "Not so *confident* now are we boys?" Taking a moment to enjoy myself and mentally photographing their terrified faces, I did my best Blackthorn act. "Did I not mention it? I'm Malakai's apprentice..."

David's mouth twitched, his eyes gazing at the immense Malakai. "*You?* Why you?" He said it in a small voice, clearly some bravado remained.

"I'm a *Blackthorn*. This is who we are and believe me, the Spells he's already shown me... *Reptlylidiulis!*"

From the ends of my hands grew a green and brown light that morphed into a giant snake. Giant neon fangs snapped the air in the front of them.

"*AHHHH!*" they all cried, stepping back.

KERKALCULEVREO

Revealing spell

This spell allows one to make an object reveal any information it is carrying like important memories.

Avis, Robin and Tina perform Kerkalculevreo upon Malakai's amulet in their first year, and it revealed portions of Malakai's time at Hailing Hall and him trying to get rid of the amulet.

PERCEIVUS

Offensive spell

Used to stun and confuse. Takes the form of red and black smoke, in an arrow/mushroom shape.

 "Your parents convinced me to leave you be," he

sighed deeply and carried on. "Perhaps they are traitors, very clever traitors..." He kept talking slowly, breathlessly. "Seventh sons are rare, very rare. I can control everyone, using this book, except seventh sons. Your *true names* are unknown..." Then his whole tone changed, suddenly he let out a cry: "*PERCEIVUS!*" He cried. Streaks of red and black smoke shot across the room at me.

"STEVE MALCOLM!" I called. The red and black smoke Spell squirmed to the floor like a writhing snake.

FLUTTERYOUT

Offensive spell

It's very hard to avoid being hit by a Flutteryout, as they are almost invisible — in a darkened room however, they will appear as a white light. However, they are so fast, they can even catch a very powerful wizard out.

> Ernie crept down through darkness. The next second he stood, facing a large man dressed all in black, face long and skeletal with blue glowing eyes that came to rest on Ernie, who raised his hands quickly. Red, green and gold flashes scorched the air. Malakai flapped and the light burst in a shard of sparks. The two foes faced each other. With a long skeletal hand, Malakai pinned Ernie to the floor. A very large book with a brown cover, older than time itself, stood on a gold mantle.
>
> "How dare you! Coming here and interfering in *my* business!" Malakai cried.

Ernie looked charged, he whispered something and vanished, like a mirage. The next moment he was behind Malakai. "*Flutteryout!*" he cried.

Malakai flew into the opposite wall. Ernie grabbed the book, which fizzed and made horrible cracking noises. Malakai roared.

"Give that back! Don't you dare!" A whistling lit the air. Ernie stood terrified, unable to move. The next moment he was bound by thick red snaking, chains. Malakai took the book and placed it back on the mantle carefully. Ernie struggled against the expanding chains.

Percival

Charm spell
This spell charms a doors lock to open.

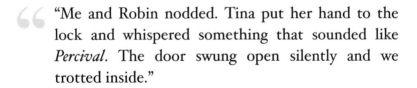

"Me and Robin nodded. Tina put her hand to the lock and whispered something that sounded like *Percival*. The door swung open silently and we trotted inside."

BERATATER-LUT

Weather Spell
Avis uses this to cause a distraction in the Riptide Match, so he can quickly make his escape and to find Malakai.

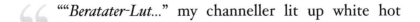

""*Beratater-Lut...*" my channeller lit up white hot

with the effort of the Spell as directly above the pitch, a bright orange circle appeared. Then, a spectacular thunderstorm erupted above the habitat.

CRASH! BANG!

Long streaks of blue light lit up the sky, scorching across the stadium. There were muffled screams from all around the stadium as people ducked. Magisteers stood as one and raised their arms. The Centaurs and Manticores ran for cover as Magisteer Underwood began scouring the pitch for the culprit - thinking that it must have been one of the players. I took my chance, as the bullish sixth year guarding the nearest exit left his post to help. I jumped up onto the rail and, balancing nimbly, ran all the way along to the stairs. I jumped the rickey stairs three at a time as the crowd in the stadium began to boo whomever had just ruined the game."

OTHER SPELLS MENTIONED IN THE BOOK:

According to Magisteer Yearlove, if you fuse a Dancidious and a Prohebe spell together, this will stop an attacker in their tracks. He would be right too, Dancidious would pre-empt an attack and counter it, while a Prohebe spell would enforce a rigour-mortis type effect upon the body.

TABEO-OSSA: Liquidates the bones, making someone collapse like a bag of jelly. Sometimes used by the Protectorates (Wizard Police).

IF YOU NEED to keep someone captive, to chain them up for any reason, then the go-to spell would be: ***Sanguis-Catena.*** Be careful though, you will need to repeat the spell every six hours, or it will wear off and your captor will escape. To remove it: ***Recludo-Depellerant.***

RETURIOUS-TACE-USQE-GLACIENTOR, is a bit of a mouth-full to say, but it's quite a good spell considered it was invented by a second year — Robin Wilson fused together four spells from his Spell-craft book to make something that freezes Occulus's retina, making them motionless, and easy to walk past without them sounding their alarm. `

PARTIMO-SESAMEA IS another good spell for unlocking doors — it's based on the "open-sesame" you would have heard through myths and legends of magic. It's a very old spell that almost died out, along with abracadabra, through overuse. But, it's making a comeback again. Partimo, basically translated means *open*.

A **RED MISERIA** spell is used to alert someone of your location, like a flare.

RELOVOTESSELLAREGRASSUS IS A MOUTHFUL OF A SPELL, and is used by Magisteer Yearlove to spell the flower when it took on a life of its own and tried to kill Avis mid-lesson. It's a concoc-tion of flames that would kill a plant, not a person, and a charm that would kill any curse that the plant may have inside it. Like a flame doused in water.

PERGOATERFERACE WAS USED in the Riptide match against the Swillows in Avis's second year. Avis asks Robin to make his injuries disappear. **Goaternut** is a spell that makes you disappear, thus, adding per and -ferace to the start and end tailor it specifically towards obscuring injuries.

SEVERSO-ZXANXIRIOUS-UNQUART-VILUNOS   (S-Z-U-V SPELL) is used by Avis against Jasper in his second year. It's a powerful offensive spell, that explodes like a grenade. The only place Avis could have seen this spell used is by his family.

JARRED IS an enchantment put upon something that makes it unsayable, and sometimes unthinkable. But most commonly saying something is Jarred, refers to a name that cannot be said. When Avis discovers Malakai's True Name, and tries to say it, he cannot, it's Jarred.

A DIFFERENCE IN SPELLING

Perhaps a spells page is the best time to mention something else that is different about the magical world. Just like America and the U.K share the same language, but spell words differently; like color and colour. So to does the magical world.

FOR INSTANCE when talking about being thrown out of school, in English we spell this: ***expelled***. However, in the SMK's (Seven Magical Kingdoms) this is spelt: ***exspelled***.

SO IF YOU notice any strange spellings, put it down to that.

ALSO YOU MUST ALSO REMEMBER that these books are written by a teenage boy, the spelling and grammar are not always going to be top-notch!

❧ 27 ❧

SHRUNKEN HEADS

S hrunken heads are used when someone is under great threat of being attacked. It serves as a shield of armour might, in deflecting any wayward spells or hexes that may be heading towards one. Avis experienced them first hand, when given one in his first year when he is let out of the turret and back into the main school after being accused of trying to kill Hunter. They are small, about the size of a tennis ball, with string sewn through their lips and eyes. When needed, they are thrown up into the air, the string falls away and their eyes open. They sit in mid-air floating just behind ones right shoulder.

ORIGINATING FROM MODAFAFA, and their tribal magics a great trade in Shrunken Heads was made towards the end of the 18th century as times became dangerous. No one would dare venture out into the big cities without one. There became such a shortage of them, that one reached as high as 2000 gold pieces, which back then was enough to buy a mansion.

Magisteer Simone held her hand out. On it, was a tiny shrivelled head on a string.

"You will be accompanied by a Shrunken Head to protect you from Spells, Hexes, Curses and bullish behaviour from others while we ascertain what *really happened...*" She chucked the head to me. It was small, with flaky skin and rough hair, it's eyes and mouth sealed by thread. "Put it round your neck, then make your way down to Lunch." This had to go round my neck? Ergh.

"What happens?" I said. "If someone does attack me or whatever?" I saw her smile as if imagining it.

"You're a Blackthorn? And you don't know about Shrunken Heads? Dear, oh dear..." she tutted and vanished from the room leaving me standing, stranded in a prison cell I didn't want to leave.

I put the horrible Shrunken Head around my

neck. It hung limp for a bit, then the thread in its eyes and mouth disappeared with a *poof*. It groaned and began mumbling strange words to itself. The string around my neck disappeared in a short blaze of orange as the head floated up just behind my left shoulder, where it stayed muttering to itself.

"Hello?" I said. But it ignored me, eyes shut.

❧ 28 ❧

MARK OF THE 7TH SON

The myth of a seventh son stretches throughout cultures and boundaries. It's always been thought that a seventh son has extra powers, though no one has ever actually confirmed this. But, when Malakai in the height of his power starts killing seventh sons, it adds a weight of mystery to the myth.

IF YOU STUDY the magical history, you will see that many famous Wizards, were in fact seventh sons and many died in mysterious circumstances.

AVIS OFTEN WONDERS why he is different to his family — they are evil and he is not. But why? Perhaps it has something to do with the fact that he is the seventh son in the family? He has six older brothers.

BUT THE MYTH GOES FURTHER, if you are the seventh son of a seventh son, then you are meant to have incredible powers.

WHEN AVIS, Robin and Ernie enter the room that they suspect Malakai has been hiding in, they find it littered with dirt and debris, as many old classrooms are, but upon the wall was the same strange mark that Avis kept seeing (pic below). Upon Avis's channeller was the *mark*, so to on Jasper's channeller, also on the urn of ashes that Avis's grandfather was in, and the incense holder that contained the Djinn Burrows inside.

""*Prafulgeo-Lamas*," Ernie whispered, as a circle of soft blue flame attached to the ceiling illuminating the room. "He's not here..." said Ernie, voice uncertain.

Robin, behind me whimpered slightly — I moved tentatively behind Ernie, scanning every corner and crevice of this dirty, disgusting room. The blue light above illuminated a floor thick with black dirt, dead rats, and upturned classroom furniture. "What's he doing in here?" said Robin. "Shedding his poxy skin or something?" Robin picked up a pile of crusty black dirt.

I searched the room — this was perfect, all I had to do was show the Lily this room and it would be proof that Malakai was in the school. I was saved! There was a small scuttling noise, it made my heart leap into my throat. I turned quickly, arms out.

"It's just a sprat," said Ernie without turning. "Come on, we don't know when he might be back."

"It's an old disused classroom," said Ernie, peering up at a huge blackboard that had a large selection of runes in chalk on it. "Runes... hold on, they're not runes! Avis, your gonna want to look at this..." I turned and looked — plastered across the blackboard in every available space was: *Kill Avis Blackthorn! Kill Avis Blackthorn! Kill Avis Blackthorn!* I stepped back, feeling a little giddy.

"Jeez," said Ernie. "He *really* wants you dead." I turned away and looked for more evidence, swallowing the fear that was plastered to my insides. Then Ernie scoffed, looking up at something. "He's quite the artist, looks like he's graffiti'ed the wall for some reason."

"How do you know it was him that did it?" said Robin rather impatiently, edging towards the door. "This looks like a rune classroom, or *was*, it could have been anyone in here."

"Because it's recent," said Ernie. "You can tell by the soft glow of the magic used to create it."

I dropped a flaky old book and turned to see

what they were jabbering about — and I almost suffered a heart attack. "*Ah*," was all I could manage. On the wall, painted in thick black paint — was the exact same rune that was on my pendant.

"What is it?" said Robin, his beady eyes flickering around the room.

I pointed up at it. "It's the same rune that's on my pendant. Exactly the same one."

"I'm sure it's nothing," said Ernie. "It doesn't look like any rune I've ever seen. Anyway look we need to get out of here and let the Lily know...""

THE VOLUMINO

After Avis's debacle involving setting the Djinn free in the school in exchange for the magical jumper, he is tasked with finding the Djinn and recapturing it. Magisteer Straker is, unwillingly, tasked with helping Avis. And so starts many long night searching the school, fruitlessly in search of it. But during this time, Avis and Straker, strangely, build up an understanding. So much so, that Straker unveils a modified Occulus that he calls a Volumino. It's an eye ball with metallic wings that flies ahead of them, beaming out a bright blue ray of light which scans every part of the corridor ahead of them searching specifically for discarnate beings. And then, even more strangely, at the end of the year, Magisteer Straker gives Avis the Volumino as a present.

"Straker pulled a tiny silver ball out of his pocket, then threw it into the air. It split into two pieces, the parted silver crescents acting like tiny wings beating ferociously. In the middle of these wings was a pure white eyeball. It seemed to awaken, the retina swinging into motion and darting around as the wings beat hard. From out of the retina a bright blue light, laser focused in a concentrated beam, burst outwards. The blue light began scanning every nook and cranny.

"It's an Occulus' that I changed..." said Straker. "It will scan the area up ahead for us with its laser light focus, I reduced the eye in size, changed its sight, upscaled it so that it can spot invisibles, spirits... Djinn. It's also invisible to them, but not to us."

"Woah..." I said amazed that anyone could just create something like this.

"I call it the Volucer-Illumino or the Volumino for short."

"It's amazing," I'd never seen anything like it, a flying eyeball that hunted for spirits? It flew far ahead of us down the corridor, its bright blue beam shooting into crevices and crannies, leaving no space unchecked."

❧ 30 ❧

THE MAGICAL JUMPER

In Avis's second year at Hailing Hall they go to the Happendance Carnival and while out looking at the stalls, Avis spots an antique with the strange mark (mark of the seventh son) on it. So he buys it and takes it back. He soon discovers that it contains a Djinn, and in lessons with Magisteer Yearlove soon realises how powerful and rare it is to have one of these — as it can grant him a wish... anything he wants.

The Djinn, Burrows released from the Incense holder grants Avis a wish and thus, knits him a magical, multicolour jumper...

AVIS, against Robin's advice, goes up to the clock tower and performs the spell that will release the Djinn and grant Avis a wish. When the Djinn comes out as expected, Avis wishes to be popular, to be liked. And so the Djinn knits Avis a jumper of different colours. Whenever he wears it, he soon realises that people respond to him differently, he is no longer tarnished with the Blackthorn name, people like him.

But as with every wish, there is a bite in the tail. Avis snags the jumper on a spiked boulder illusion from Magisteer Simone's room and this causes the magic within the jumper to go weird. And soon people start going mad around Avis and the jumper, competing and fighting for his attention. It becomes unbearable.

Robin is immune to the jumpers effects, if he wears his special spectacles. But it soon gets Avis into more trouble...

AND IT IS HERE, when Avis is about to enter the Lily's office, expecting to be exspelled, when something strange happens...

> "This is it then," said Robin robotically. "Good luck." I nodded once, unable to speak. For my fate was waiting inside that room. But as I began to walk, I felt something tingling in my arms. Then my chest. Then... my neck. I stopped walking, as I tried to work out what was happening. It was the jumper, it was tightening! The strands were contracting like

a snake, squeezing me tighter and tighter. I bent forwards with the pain, all the air being squashed from my lungs.

Robin stopped dead staring at me. "What's happened?!" he cried. "AVIS!" All I could manage was gasping breaths as the jumper began strangling me with its thick woollen hands! I grabbed fistfuls of wool and pulled. But it was too strong — grip harder than steel. "HELP! *HEEEELLLPPP!*" Robin cried.

Running footsteps echoed up the corridor, then voices and blurred faces. "Oh no!" cried the voices.

Robin cried. "Please, you've got to help him, I don't know what to do!"

"We must help Avis Blackthorn!" they said.

"I want to save him!" said another arriving on the scene.

"No!" cried the sixth years. "We are saving him, now go away."

I couldn't hear the rest, my consciousness was fading. They were arguing about who would be the one to save me, as I lay struggling for breath. I started to see stars, and hazy colours. The energy was fading out of me as all noise and light began to dissipate.

A flash illuminated the hallway. I felt the strangling hands fall away. I could breath again — great lungfuls of air swept into my body. I could see again... the tall, white outline of the Lily stared down at me.

THE WIZARDING SPORT OF RIPTIDE

Riptide is a wizarding sport. It grew naturally out from duelling hundreds of years ago, and formed into the sport that we know today. Clans, tribes or factions of neighbouring towns would compete against one another to get a flag to one side of the pitch, before the other team, all whilst duelling each other with spells and magic. Later on the flag, turned into a ball or a flounder — so named as the first ball was made of Flounder skin (a ratty, ferret-type magical animal).

THESE DAYS, Riptide is worth big money. They have the Merlin Premier League and several leagues below that, as well as an All Kingdoms Cup, and a World Cup amongst the different nations.

THE RULES OF RIPTIDE

Magisteer Partington, their form tutor, explains for the first time, the *rules of Riptide*:

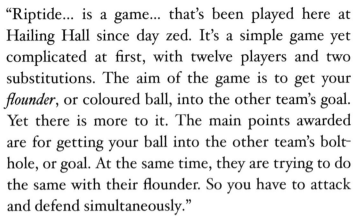

"Riptide... is a game... that's been played here at Hailing Hall since day zed. It's a simple game yet complicated at first, with twelve players and two substitutions. The aim of the game is to get your *flounder*, or coloured ball, into the other team's goal. Yet there is more to it. The main points awarded are for getting your ball into the other team's bolt-hole, or goal. At the same time, they are trying to do the same with their flounder. So you have to attack and defend simultaneously."

This picture of a chequered pitch drew itself on the board behind Partington. Twelve dots moved around on the pitch, throwing a blue and a red ball to each other. "When you get your ball in the other team's bolt hole, you score a point..." this jet of red light shot into the air from the bolt hole. "And light shoots out into the sky. The goal which we call a bolt-hole is a magical stone, looks like a stone fountain, you must get the ball in there." I was taking notes and trying to keep up furiously with what he was saying. "But... you can also score points by stealing the other teams ball and putting in their own goal." Everyone was scribbling down notes now.

"There are seven allowed Spells in Riptide, which is more like twenty-three if you include Counter-Spells. These seven Spells are for offence, defence, effecting your ball and changing yourself or the environment. The main two you will want to use are..." Partington counted on his fingers. "Raising an opponent into the air and the Spell for breaking the Spell that raises you into the air. We will cover these shortly. When you raise an opponent into the air, if they are airborne for longer than *three seconds,* then they are out of the game. If you escape within three seconds, you're safe. It's all governed by Magic, so there's no cheating. When you are eliminated, you will shoot off, back to the game bench.

"Now, the pitch. The Riptide pitch looks chequered, but it's actually what we call an *illusory-habitat*, write that down. It means that the pitch will change into a variety of set environments. So it might fill up with large rocks, good for hiding behind, or with long grass, or with trees, or with historical buildings which make for the best entertainment. It could be anything and you won't know what until you step out there and the whistle goes."

"The flounders are always red and blue. You can throw them, hide them, do whatever you want with them, as long as you get it to that bolt-hole in time. The games run for twelve minutes and there are five games a match. Extra points are earned for getting the entire opposing team into the air, no matter how many points the other team has, you win that game. But don't worry about this too much for now.

"Now, the environment has other tricks up its sleeve. Hidden around it are what we call Ornaments. It might be a vase on a fireplace in a Venetian fourteenth century setting, or a locket in a tree stump... these Ornaments have special powers that last the entirety of a game. The powers are too numerous to name, but could include - making you invisible to the opposite team, they make your ball invisible, give you flight, it could be a Spell shield... literally anything you can think of..."

SUMMARY OF THE RULES OF RIPTIDE:

- To score a goal, you must get the flounder into the other teams goal (or Bolt-Hole), which is a stone crater bowl with a big black hole in it.
- There are two flounders, red and blue, that makes it harder as you have to simultaneously attack and defend.
- You must duel against the other team, using magic to get your flounder up the pitch and into the goal.
- First team to five goals wins the game (or the best score after ten minutes).
- The best out of five games, wins the match.
- The pitch, or Habitat, takes on a multitude of different styles, so one game you can play
- The Habitat contains Ornaments, that when found can give you 'power-ups', like invisibility for your whole team, or better eye-sight or a weather change, its usually, but not always, very useful and can almost guarantee your side a great advantage if you find one.
- If you spell another player into the air and they are air-borne for longer than 3 seconds, they are out of the game. If one team spells every single member off the pitch, they gain whats called a Libero-Manus and win the game automatically.

THE SEVEN MAIN SPELLS OF RIPTIDE:

PASANTHEDINE

To raise another into the air

    This is used most commonly as this is the spell that can get another spelled out of the game.

KADRIEPOP

To get down from a Pasanthedine

This is the spell you need to use to come back down again after being spelled into the air by Pasanthedine. You need to waive your hands around in a particular motion so as to ensure you get a clean landing.

GOATERNUT

"The chameleon spell."

This spell makes you almost invisible. I say almost because you actually become more like a chameleon, merging in with the surroundings.

YOU MAY BE THINKING, *why not have this spell on constantly to avoid detection?* Well, for a few reasons: firstly, your team won't be able to see you to pass you the flounder, and secondly, it only lasts for thirty seconds before wearing off.

Robin and Avis demonstrating Goaternut in class.

SEVHURTON

The Freeze spell.

If you want to freeze someone solid, then use this spell. You can freeze someone solid to stop them from spelling you, or you can freeze their spell in mid-air. The uses are numerous. You can even spell the flood with ice to make it slippy.

Nouchous
The fire spell.

Opposite of the ice spell, this spell makes a ball of fire fly at your opponent. It's not enough to set them alight, unless they are doused in petrol, but it enough to hurt and knock one for six.

Zxanbatters

The Magnet Spell

This is particularly useful when playing with flounders, as you can use Zxanbatters to make the ball zap towards you if its nearby.

THIS MAKES for an interesting spectacle when several zxanbatters makes the flounder zig-zag around the pitch like a
mad wasp.

COULD YOU DO ME A FAVOUR?

Thank you so much for taking the time to read this book. I really hope you enjoyed reading it as much as I enjoyed writing it and putting in all the fabulous illustrations.

I would love to hear what you thought about it!

So, at the end of this book, if you scroll to the last page on eBook, you can leave a review. I would really appreciate it.

Yours,

Jack Simmonds
 — London, U.K.

A BIG THANK YOU

A huge and obvious thank you goes to Magda Szerszeń. Without whom, this book would not have been made. Your talent and dedication to illustration is clear and you have a big future.

I wish you all the luck in the world.

Jack

Start reading the first book in the series for FREE. Just go to jacksimmondsbooks.com and sign up!

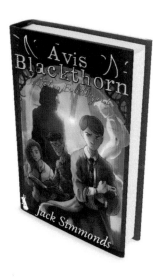

In a world of Magic... which side do you choose?

Evil = be safe.

Good = be very unsafe.

It's a dilemma 12 year old Avis Blackthorn faces. If he doesn't chose wisely, it could be his last.

Start reading now: Avis Blackthorn: Is Not an Evil Wizard!

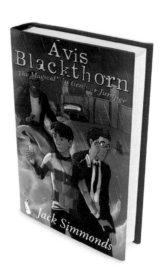

What if you found a genie and it granted you a Wish?

What would you choose...

Money, fame or love?

Start reading now: Avis Blackthorn and the Magical Multicolour
Jumper (Book 2)

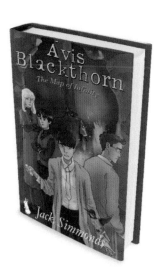

How would you feel if someone made you Evil?

Enter the Belafonte twins...

...two of the most **evil** twins, with a terrible reputation, have joined the school... and they're here for a reason.

Start reading now:

Avis Blackthorn: The Map of Infinity (Book 3)

You borrow a priceless magical artefact... then lose it.

What do you do?

Start reading now:

Avis Blackthorn and the Ring of Enchantment (Prequel)

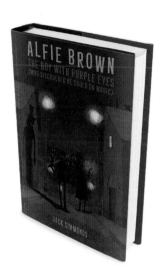

What would you do if you discovered you could do real magic?

... and had purple eyes.

Start reading now:

Alfie Brown: The Boy With Purple Eyes (Who Discovered He Could Do Magic) - A Novel

Printed in Poland
by Amazon Fulfillment
Poland Sp. z o.o., Wrocław